Catch the Rabbit

Catch the Rabbit

LANA BASTAŠIĆ

Translated by the author

PICADOR

First published 2021 by Picador
an imprint of Pan Macmillan
The Smithson, 6 Briset Street, London EC1M 5NR
EU representative: Macmillan Publishers Ireland Limited,
Mallard Lodge, Lansdowne Village, Dublin 4
Associated companies throughout the world
www.panmacmillan.com

ISBN 978-1-5290-3960-3

1 3 5 7 9 8 6 4 2

A CIP catalogue record for this book is available from the British Library.

Typeset in Photina by Jouve (UK), Milton Keynes
Printed and bound by CPI Group (UK) Ltd, Croydon, CR0 4YY

MIX
Paper from
responsible sources
FSC® C116313

Visit **www.picador.com** to read more about all our books
and to buy them. You will also find features, author interviews and
news of any author events, and you can sign up for e-newsletters
so that you're always first to hear about our new releases.

'I could tell you my adventures—beginning from this morning,' said Alice a little timidly: 'but it's no use going back to yesterday, because I was a different person then.'

'Explain all that,' said the Mock Turtle.

'No, no! The adventures first,' said the Gryphon in an impatient tone: 'explanations take such a dreadful time.'

— Lewis Carroll,
Alice's Adventures in Wonderland

one

to start from the beginning. You have someone and then you don't. And that's the whole story. Except *you* would say you can't *have* a person. Or should I say *she?* Perhaps that's better, you'd like that. To be a *she* in a book. All right, then.

She would say you can't have a person. But she would be wrong. You *can* own people for embarrassingly little. Only she likes to think of herself as the general rule for the workings of the whole cosmos. And the truth is you *can* have someone, just not her. You can't have Lejla. Unless you finish her off, put her in a nice frame, and hang her on the wall. Although, is it really still us once we stop, once we freeze for the picture? One thing I know for sure: stopping and Lejla never went together well. That's why she is a blur in every single photograph. She could never stop.

Even now, within this text, I can almost feel her fidget. If she could, she would sneak between two sentences like a moth between two slats of a venetian blind, and would finish my story off from the inside. She would change into the sparkly rags she always liked, lengthen her legs, enhance her breasts, add some waves to her hair. Me she would disfigure, leaving a single lock of hair on my square head; she would give me a speech impediment, make my left leg limp, think up an inherent deformity so I keep dropping the pencil. Perhaps she would take it one step further, she is capable of such villainy – she wouldn't even mention me at all. Turn me into an unfinished sketch. You would do that, wouldn't you? Sorry – *she*. She would do that if she were here. But *I* am the one telling the story. I can do whatever I want with her. *She* can't do anything. *She* is three hits on the keyboard. I could throw the laptop into the mute Viennese Danube tonight and she would be gone, her fragile pixels would bleed into the cold water and empty everything she ever was out into the Black Sea, dodging Bosnia like a countess dodges a beggar on her way to the opera. I could end her with this sentence so that she no longer is, she would disappear, become a pale face in a prom photo, forgotten in an urban legend from high school, mentioned in some drunk moron's footnote where he boasts of all those he *had* before he *settled down*; she would be barely detectable in the little heap of earth we left there behind her house next to the cherry tree. I could kill her with a full stop.

I choose to continue because I can. At least here I feel safe from her subtle violence. After a whole decade, I go back to my language – her language, and all the other languages I voluntarily abandoned, like one would a violent husband one afternoon in Dublin. After all these years, I'm not sure which language that is. And all that because of what? Because of the totally ordinary Lejla Begić, in her old sneakers with straps and jeans with, for God's sakes, diamanté on the butt.

What happened between us? Does it matter? Good stories are never about what happens anyway. Pictures are all that's left, like pavement paintings, years fall over them like rain. But our beginning was never a simple, silent observer of chronology. Our beginning came and went several times, pulling on my sleeve like a hungry puppy. *Let's go. Let's start again.* We would constantly start and end, she would sneak into the fabric of the everyday like a virus. Enters Lejla, exits Lejla. I can start anywhere, really. Dublin, St. Stephen's Green, for instance. The cell phone vibrating in my coat pocket. Unknown number. Then I press the damn button and say *yes* in a language not my own.

'Hello, you.'

After twelve years of complete silence, I hear her voice again. She speaks quickly, as if we parted yesterday, without the need to bridge gaps in knowledge, friendship, and chronology. I can only utter one word, *Lejla*. As always, she won't shut up. She mentions a restaurant, a job in a restaurant, some guy whose name I've never heard before. She mentions Vienna. And I, still, just *Lejla*. Her name was seemingly harmless – a little shoot amidst dead earth. I plucked it out of my lungs thinking it meant nothing. Lejla. But along with the innocent stem, the longest and thickest roots came spilling out from the mud, an entire forest of letters, words, and sentences. A whole language buried deep inside me, a language that had waited patiently for that little word to stretch its numb limbs and rise as if it had never slept at all. Lejla.

*

'Where did you get this number?' I ask. I'm standing in the middle of the park, stopped right in front of an oak, paralyzed, as if waiting for the tree to step aside and let me past.

'What does it matter?' she answers and goes on with her monologue. 'Listen, you gotta come pick me up . . . Can you hear me? The connection's bad.'

'Pick you up? I don't understand. What . . .'

'Yeah, pick me up. I'm still in Mostar.'

Still. During all those years of our friendship she had never once mentioned Mostar. We had never been there, either, and now it somehow represented an indisputable, common-knowledge fact.

'In Mostar? What are you doing in Mostar?'

I'm still looking at the tree, counting the years in my head. Forty-eight seasons without her voice. I know I'm going somewhere, my route has something to do with Michael, and the curtains, and the pharmacy, but all that has come to a standstill now. Lejla showed up, said cut, and everything froze. Trees, trams, people. Like tired actors.

'Listen, Mostar is a long story . . . You still drive, right?'

'I do, but I don't get what . . . Do you know I'm in Dublin?'

I keep looking around me, afraid that someone would hear me. Words fall out of my mouth and stick to my coat like burrs. When was the last time I spoke *that language*?

'Yeah, you're very important,' Lejla says, ready to devalue the entirety of what I might have lived in her absence. 'Living on an island, probably reading that boring big-ass book all day long, having brunch with your brainy friends, right? Awesome. Anyway, listen . . . You gotta come get me as soon as you can. I gotta go to Vienna and these morons took my license and nobody gets that I have to . . .'

'Lejla,' I try to interrupt her. Even after all these years it is perfectly clear to me what's going on. It's that particular logic of hers that says gravity is to blame if someone pushes you down a flight of stairs, that all trees were planted so that she could take a piss behind them, and that all roads, no matter how meandering and long, have one connecting dot, the same knot – her. Rome is a joke.

'Listen, I don't have a lot of time. I really have no one else to ask, everyone's bullshitting me with how busy they are, not that I have a lot of friends here to be honest, and Dino can't drive 'cause of his knee . . .'

'Who's Dino?'

'. . . so I was thinking you could fly to Zagreb this weekend and get on a bus, though maybe Dubrovnik would be better.'

'Lejla, I'm in Dublin. I can't just pick you up in Mostar and drive you to Vienna. Are you insane?'

She's quiet for a while; the air leaves her nostrils and hits the receiver. She sounds like a patient mother doing her best not to slap a little kid. After some moments of her heavy breathing and my staring at the stubborn oak, she says, 'You have to.'

There's nothing threating in it, nothing hostile. It sounds more like a doctor telling you to quit smoking. And the *have to* doesn't bother me, nor the way she's called me twelve years later without a single *how are you*, nor how she sneered at the whole life I had invented in between. After all, that's classic Lejla. But the fact that somewhere in her voice there was absolute certainty I would say yes, that I had no choice, that my fate had been sealed before I answered the damn phone – that I find belittling.

I hang up and put the cell phone in my pocket. No way. Even the gods, no matter how primitive and mindless they might be, grant us the right of free will. I look at the tree and breathe slowly; I don't trust that air anymore. I have polluted it with *my language*. I try to summarize what just happened, recounting the whole scene the way I will deliver it to Michael when I get home. Can you believe this, I'll say, this friend from Bosnia called me today and asked . . . I'm planning the words in a foreign language, weave and twist them so tightly that not a speck of light can slip through the threads. And just when I think I know how to narrate her, I know how to deprive her of all meaning, just when it seems like some cars have thundered in the distance, and people are once again moving in my peripheral vision, and the wind is back in the top of that oak tree – she calls me again.

'Sara, listen to me. Please,' she says, more quietly. *Saro.* My name, deformed with the vocative case I had forgotten about, sounds like an echo in an abandoned well. I know her. She's that innocent stem again, someone whose hands are so delicate you'd let her hold your own brain.

'Lejla, I'm in Dublin. I live with someone. I have responsibilities. I can't go to Mostar. OK?'

'But you have to.'

'You vanish for over ten years. You don't answer my emails. You don't contact me in any way. For all I knew, you could have been buried in some . . . shithole. The last time I saw you, you told me to go fuck myself.'

'I didn't tell you to . . .'

'OK, great. Whatever. And now you call me and expect me to simply . . .'

'Sara, Armin is in Vienna.'

All the birds in the tree above my head turn to stone. The earth is loose below me; I'll stay here, planted in front of the oak tree, which will be free to run away. I can feel two crows eyeing me from a nearby willow. I almost wish they would dive onto my head and gouge out my eyes and ears and tongue. But they can't – they're made of stone.

'What did you say?' I ask. Now I'm whispering. I'm scared to scare off her voice; it would run away from me like a cockroach.

'Armin's in Vienna,' she repeats. 'You gotta come pick me up.'

I go into the first Starbucks I pass and buy a plane ticket to Zagreb online, Munich connection, 586 euros.

[She never wanted to talk about her brother. But that night something was different, something broke inside her like a feeble straw fence. It was the first Monday after college graduation, one of those weeks when your life is supposed to start, or at least another stage of it. I had waited the whole weekend to feel different. Nothing happened. Like someone had sold me bad weed.

We were sitting on the couch in her room. Stray cats howled painfully in the street.

'Twenty marks,' she said, stroking the brown plush cover that stretched tantalizingly between her and me. 'The man came and changed it.'

'What color was it before?' I asked. It must have been the hundredth time I'd been in her room, yet I couldn't recall that couch in any other shade but brown.

'Beige, of course,' she said. 'Don't you remember?'

To me this was unacceptable: her and beige. She was never one for beige. Those people are silent and ordinary. I didn't dare ask about the other colors that, I was sure, had stained the pale couch during the years I hadn't visited. I was quiet most of the time. Nervous. After that day on the island she had stopped talking to me. Three years of college without a single word from her. And now, out of nowhere, I was there on her couch, had given in to the first call, embarrassingly ready to accept anything.

We were drinking wine, even though I didn't feel like alcohol. Lejla poured me a full glass and said firmly, yet gently, 'Drink.' And so I drank. Wine or something else, I can't remember. I only know her black mane was surprisingly heavy on my shoulder. I say 'black' because to me she has always been the scruffy raven from high school, regardless of all the bleach she now used as camouflage. I remember her eyes flickered with the reflection of a tiny window and the thick darkness spilled behind it. I remember her handsome brother observing us from the only photograph in the room. Time had faded his cheeks, his sky, his swimming trunks. And what else? What more? What was the carpet like? Did she even have a carpet? Did the ceiling still have that hideous lampshade with fake black pearls she had bought in Dalmatia? Or had she gotten rid of that? How should I know? It doesn't matter. I can't explain Lejla by describing her room. It would be like describing an apple using mathematics. I can only remember her heavy head and how her painted toenail peeked through the hole in her sock. I remember her brother. If it hadn't been for that photo, there would have been no life in that room.

Her mother kept banging pots around in the kitchen. A thin bit of wall separated us. I think I said something stupid, something that seemed funny at the time, like *Aren't you too old to have a mother in the kitchen?* or something like that, and that Lejla smiled – after all, I had one too. It seems like our town was that way back then – full of grown children and hunched, gray-haired mothers.

Why had I come that night? I wanted to ignore her and not jump at the first bone she tossed my way. But that morning she had found her rabbit dead on the cold bathroom tiles. I say cold – someone will correct that at some point. They will say I wasn't there to touch them, how do I know they were cold? But I know a bit about that rabbit of hers, and the bathroom, and those feverish hands which always felt like they were hovering around 38°. I know she was probably wearing those puffy apricot-colored slippers and that she crouched down to touch the corpse. I know she thought *corpse*. I can see the bruises on her bony knees.

He never had an official name. He was Hare, Rabbit, or Bunny, depending on Lejla's mood. I remember we buried him in her backyard, under the old cherry tree, which she claimed was radioactive. I told her this was the first time I was burying an animal.

'That's not true. What about your turtles?' she asked me almost desperately. I remember how her hands were full of her dead Rabbit and how she held him, like a precious dowry, in a blue garbage bag.

'The turtles don't count,' I said. 'They were like five to six centimeters across, like *uštipci*. A few shovels. That hardly counts as serious undertaker experience.'

'So, what are we gonna do?'

The neighbor lent us a shovel thinking we were planting strawberries. It wasn't a big tool, just a toy for adults really, light in the hand. It took me forever to dig a hole big enough. I wanted to tell her off for the corpse's bulk, but I swallowed my criticism that day. She looked small and frightened, as if she had fallen out of some nest prematurely.

We laid the bag with Bunny in the little plot. Tiny roots crawled up from the earth, embracing the corpse with their thin fingers, and then pulled it deep down into their cold womb. When it was over, I laid two white stones on the ground to mark the grave, which quite predictably made her roll her eyes.

'Go on, say something,' she said.

'Say what?'

'Whatever. You built him a monument, so a couple of words are in order.'

'Why me?'

'You're the poet.'

How vicious, I thought. One pretty lousy poetry collection and now I was supposed to deliver eulogies to poisoned rabbits. But given the lost look in her eyes and her white hands tragically empty of her Bunny, I coughed and, staring blandly at the two silent stones, pulled out the appropriate lines from some past life or other:

'Speak low and little.

So I don't hear you.

Especially about how smart I was.

What did I want? My hands are empty,

they lie sad on the cover.

What did I think about? On my lips, dryness and estrangement.

Did I live anything?

Oh, how sweetly I slept!'

And that's when she cried, I think. Perhaps it was me, I'm not sure. It was dark; perhaps her eyes just sparkled in the streetlight. If she is reading this, she will be pissed; she will call me a sentimental cow, because she never cries. Whatever the case, the verses worked – they did a better job of closing an unmarked chapter than a mere college degree.

My conscience was bothering me because I had made her believe the poem was mine. But in that moment, with dead Hare under the ground and Lejla above it, the idea of authorship made little sense to me. Verses were like runaway brides, not bound to Álvaro de Campos – who never existed in the first place, just like those strawberries – free from me and Lejla, free from the heap of cold earth with two stony eyes, free to *be* in one moment, and in the next to stop.

I can't remember whether we returned the shovel to the neighbor, whether we said anything else or not. I only know that later that night her head was heavy on my inadequate shoulder and how I cursed both that shoulder and the brown couch cover which had hardened into asphalt between us. We were looking at her pale brother contained inside four paper edges while her mother banged on in the kitchen.

Lejla said, 'She still has a photo of Tito. It's in the pantry, behind the *turšija* jar. If you look closely, you can see his eye between two pieces of paprika.'

I laughed, though I didn't feel like it. I always found them unbearable – those silent nostalgiacs and the cocoon in which they go on living better, happier versions of their lives in some country where strawberries grow forever and rabbits don't die. A country they could describe as perfect because they deprived us of the possibility to test that claim. I have heard her mother many more times than I have seen her. That night was the same. After a while, the pots went quiet – she laid her trombones down.

Lejla looked at the books lying on the shelf next to the photo of her brother, shut her made-up eyelids, and whispered: '*I watched it die.*'

I looked at her in confusion. She opened her eyes and, noticing my lost expression, laughed and said, 'One point for me.' When she realized that I still didn't understand what was going on, she rolled her eyes and added, '*It is swollen now, like a corpse.*' That's when I understood. It was our private game: one of us would spit out a forgotten quote taken from one of the books in sight, and the other would have to guess the title. But I couldn't understand why she'd remembered our almost forgotten ritual at that precise moment. We had played with quotes at the beginning of college, back when we thought it was enough to say clever words so that people would think you understood them. But we were no longer those people. College was out of our lives – for me like a lover I had overestimated for four years, for her like a painful vaccine someone else had told her was necessary. To Lejla, that game had always been just a more sophisticated version of hide and seek. 'Words are empty anyway,' she had once told me during a morphology exam. But that night she needed words, at least like a placebo, so I followed the rules obligingly.

'*No, it has not shrunk,*' I whispered, '*cold and empty it looks much bigger than before.*'

'Dark,' Lejla said.

'What?'

'*Dark* and empty.'

'Yes . . . Dark and empty. *The Travelogues.*'

Once I had offered the satisfactory answer and she nodded in acceptance, I closed my eyes and pressed her warm hand as if to save it from the brown plush and its charlatan beige past. It calmed me to see that she was still able to play, to resurrect quotes from some books she pretended not to like and share them with me as if she hadn't ignored me for three years. I wasn't angry. I was happy she could still believe in beauty after she had witnessed death crucified across bathroom tiles.

That was the first time she asked me that vile question.

'When are you gonna write a poem about me?'

I opened my eyes and sat up straight. I had known her for longer than I had had my period and this surprised me anyway.

'I'm sure you still write them. After that morbid book. Right? Admit it,' she said, suddenly making me feel ashamed, as if writing poetry was the same as hiding a bottle of *rakija* in a paper bag and sleeping under a bridge.

'I do,' I said. It was past ten p.m. The pots from the kitchen had long been quiet. I knew I should have gone home after the funeral. Nothing good can happen after you bury somebody's pet.

'So, why don't you write a poem about me? What's wrong with me?'

'What do you want,' I asked, 'a fucking Balašević ballad?'

I felt bad about it later. I should have said *yeah, sure,* and after a couple of days she would have forgotten that she'd ever asked, or would have laughed off her silly request, adding she'd rather die and rot than play someone's muse. But I couldn't help it. Not that my poetry was any good, but Lejla's absence from that part of my life – the way she had diligently ignored the whole endeavor including launches, reviews, and awards – hurt like a dangerous growth in the middle of my body. No, I wouldn't let her get away with this. Even if it had been her mother that she had buried that day, she wouldn't humiliate me in such a banal way. Anyone else, a beggar in the street, could have asked the same thing, and I would have believed his request was genuine. But not her. For Lejla, life was a rabid fox coming at night to steal your chickens. Writing about life meant staring at the slaughtered bird the next day, forever unable to catch the beast at its crime. Above all, it seemed she could never grasp why anyone in their right mind would sit down and write poems. Even less so, why I, in that place and that time, would ever choose to spend my nights that way. And now, after a lifelong policy of demeaning the only somewhat successful venture in my altogether unspectacular life, she was sitting there, on her fake-brown couch, with her fake-blonde hair, insulting me. Well, hell no.

'Geez, Sara,' she said and stood up. 'I was joking.'

She wasn't angry, just tired. If you ask Lejla, poetry isn't even worth fighting over. She went to the shelf, took the photo of her brother, and wiped the glass with the end of her sleeve.

'He didn't wanna draw me, either,' she said, putting the photo back in its place. Then she looked at me all wide-eyed as if she had suddenly remembered something.

'Have I ever told you how he touched a painting?'

I was quiet, all of a sudden completely redundant on her couch, the way one slipper loses its point entirely when it's not paired up. She obviously didn't need an interlocutor, only an ear to empty herself into, like an animal before it's stuffed. She said *he*. The first time after that terrible day on the island.

'I don't remember it,' she went on, 'I was too little. But Mom's told me the story a thousand times. We were in some museum. Armin was seven or eight, I think. I don't know. Anyway, he stood on tiptoe and touched the painting. But really . . . Fingers on the painting, you know? And then the whole show – the alarm went off, the guards running around, our parents freaking out . . .'

I was sitting on the couch saying nothing. After all, what could I say? What could anyone say? The fox had already run away, I couldn't catch it. All of a sudden words seemed false, expired, like stiff dry makeup on an old woman's face.

'But what matters is that Bunny got his epilogue,' she said and shrugged, cutting short the whole story about death, poetry, and guarded paintings. She was a simple girl again – the one that wouldn't ask for a nine in an exam, the one who prefers to drink her beer and not talk too much. A blonde girl in plastic slippers who could joke about the rabbit that, I remember clearly, she used to love more than people. A girl who doesn't know that Vienna is *swollen like a corpse*, who doesn't talk about her brother. Someone's frail, dumb muse. I couldn't stand her.

I said it was getting late and it was time for me to get going. Her mother had probably gone to bed already. She stared at me for a while – her eyes creeping about my face, from my lips to my eyebrows, as if I would change my mind if she looked long enough. I would stay, drink her wine, write her a poem – she only had to tug at the leash a bit. When nothing happened, when she realized I had really made up my mind to go home, her eyes fell off my face like a sheet falling off a statue. She walked to the door, opened it, and said, I think, I'm almost certain, though later she claimed it wasn't like that, 'Go fuck yourself.'

I finished my wine, or whatever else was in that glass, in one sip and left Lejla's room. I reached my house too soon, so I just kept on walking, as if I hadn't recognized my own front door. I walked for a long time, listening to crickets in untended hedges and wondering where moles were hiding that night and whether it was true what they said about big venomous snakes by the river. I walked until all the churches tolled five o'clock and, it seems, for a long time after that. I walked until twelve years later I reached St. Stephen's Green in Dublin, pulled the cell phone from my coat, and said her name. Yes, I mean *your* name. Then I stopped.]

two

I entered the apartment empty-handed. I was supposed to buy a new pair of curtains. And something else I had forgotten. His gray slippers greeted me at the entrance. One of them had a ripped sole. It would open and close with each step as if it had something on the tip of its tongue, but couldn't remember what. That was Michael's thirty-fifth birthday, those slippers. I got him a record too, can't remember which one. We bought red velvet cake and joked about dropping it on our way back to the apartment. We stopped in front of a pharmacy that was famous just because a fictional character had bought lemon soap there more than a hundred years ago.

'What if we got married?'

'Don't be ridiculous,' I replied. I opened the box and ran my fingers through the cold spongy body of the red cake. It was delicious.

'Happy birthday,' I said. And it stayed that way; the marriage idea had been discarded in front of the pharmacy like an ineffective pill. Mom stopped asking after a while. She came to visit just once. She slept in the bed with me while Michael was all crumpled up on the couch. She would wake up at seven in the morning and start clanking in the kitchen. I knew what she was thinking: I was filthy, I was embarrassing her all over the whole wide world. All of Ireland would find out that my mother never taught me how to clean. And I knew what Michael was thinking too. He would look at her enormous body and wonder whether that was in our genes. She had always been plump, but after Dad died she became entirely distorted. I thought of her blonde hair falling on my face when she would come tuck me in at night. Now it was nothing but a few thin tassels around the fat cheeks that merged with her neck. I remember what Michael said. 'Your mom has really pretty eyes.' The only thing left to compliment. And I hated him for it. I wanted to hug my big mother and protect her from his gaze.

It was a relief when she returned home. She bought a big pint glass with a shamrock design on it, though she never drank beer, and an ashtray with the Irish flag, though she never smoked. She got on a plane and went back to Bosnia. After a while, she stopped calling. Michael and I went back to normal. He – writing code; I – translating. No one talked of marriage, or my mother, anymore.

The first time we had sex it lasted about five minutes. He was drunk, I was tired, and his dog was whining in the corridor. Crude Dubliners kept shouting in the streets outside. Michael fell asleep the minute he tossed the condom away. I went to the bathroom to wash up. It was my first time at his place. Later it would become *our* place, even *my* place, although it was never any of those things – it belonged to a stout Irish woman in her sixties, who flirted with Michael and ignored me. But that night, after the five-minute sex, it was still just his apartment. I didn't know its corners; I stubbed my big toe. Once in the bathroom, I opened the cabinet behind the mirror and found enough painkillers to put a horse to sleep. Michael's migraines. I would get to know them later. The doctor would tell him to cut down on the computer. We would burst out laughing. But that evening it's just a bunch of pills in the bathroom of some guy I met the night before. It crossed my mind I had slept with a junkie. I would tell him that, around our fourth or fifth date. He would find it the funniest thing in the world.

How long was I sitting in that bathroom? Quite a long time. There was a silicone duck on one of the tiles. The drain was full of red hair. It hurt between my legs. I took two of his pills and borrowed a towel. The night was meant to have been better, everything had suggested a good outcome. A smart guy. Well-read. Funny. A bit weird. Likes Cohen. And then it all lasted five minutes after which the smart guy fell asleep. I was sitting in someone else's bathroom, not knowing it would be mine one day, thinking about all the Dubliners I'd slept with since I had moved there. All those condoms went through my mind. A small pool of wasted Irish genes. How did I end it with them? What did I say? This, too, I thought. I would leave the bathroom and call a cab. Never gave him my phone number. Won't bother me.

A pile of his dirty clothes on the washing machine. I pulled out a Darth Vader T-shirt from the heap and checked it out. It was huge and smelled like pot. I put it back on the pile and left the bathroom, determined to find my clothes and call the taxi. I could only find my jeans and a single sock. His dog was following me everywhere, obedient, as if I wasn't the first to be wandering around that flat in search of an exit. I was looking for my shirt in the living room which, back then, had a different table, not the one we would build together a couple of years later. That one doesn't exist yet. At that moment, I just wanted to locate my shirt, get out of that place, and pretend nothing happened. He was already snoring in the other room, wouldn't even realize I left. He could keep the other sock as a souvenir.

I found the shirt next to the TV and put it on, while considering which cab company to call, annoyed I had to spend money on other people's wheels again. And then I looked up at the shelves, and stopped. A little black book peeked out from a bunch of computer manuals. Its spine was covered in silver letters. I read *Treasure Island – R. L. Stevenson*. I stood there looking at the words. They glimmered in the streetlight that broke through the balcony. I felt the letters with my fingertips; the script bulged slightly, like a healed wound. Nothing hurt anymore – the painkiller had done the job. The dog was licking my bare foot. I was looking at that book and thought of Jim Hawkins, who was told to write down everything the way it happened, not to leave a thing out. After a while I took off all of my clothes and got back into bed with Michael.

How many years had gone by since then? From our first sex to Lejla's phone call? People died every day. How many of them had ceased to exist since we buried Rabbit? Whole lives were terminated while she and I weren't talking. While I was meeting Michael, sleeping with Michael, eating cake with

Michael, having fights with Michael, where was she? Why didn't she call me that day, or the one in front of the pharmacy, or the next one, or any other but this? Why didn't she call me before I saw that book on Michael's shelf? It's like she had known everything about my life, what would happen to me, before I knew it myself.

My ears were still full of her hoarse voice. She was older, rougher, but still with the same playful, rusty voice. I took a deep breath and unlocked the door slowly, as if hoping to discover Michael doing something unforgivable. It would be easier that way.

I didn't take my shoes off. He was sitting in the living room writing code that I never understood. I was standing at the door, behind his back, looking at neat sentences composed of numbers, letters, and signs, following one another, white on the black screen. Michael used to say that the whole world was coded. That I wasn't aware that behind my translation software, my favorite magazines, my playlists of old music, there was a whole language unintelligible to me. I was standing there looking at the bunch of symbols and wondering whom he would create a world for that day. Would he, unconsciously, help someone finish a Ph.D., kill a monster in a video game or, who knows, write a suicidal message with a new word-processing program? That hunched man in a large checkered sweater – whose god was he?

My hand was still in my coat pocket; I was squeezing the cell phone. *Armin is in Vienna.* I didn't think I'd be able to pack and go to the airport if my fingers dropped that phone. I would drop Lejla along with it, and Armin, and Vienna. But what would happen to the hunched god in the checkered sweater? Not a big deal – Zagreb, Mostar, Vienna. Not the end of the world. A couple of weeks. Maybe a month if I decide to stay longer. The phone was getting hot in my fist. Bosnia. Lejla. That's not a two-week holiday after which you come home and go to bed with Michael. That's like going back to heroin. I had already gotten myself dirty with my mother tongue.

I approached him from the back and took his headphones off his head, startling him. My palms rested on his shoulders. At the same time, I could feel the ease of such a well-known gesture, and the certainty that this time something was different.

'It's just me,' I said.

'You get the curtains?' he asked, still looking at the screen.

'No,' I said. English fell down my stomach brick by brick.

'I'll go tomorrow,' he said, 'if you don't mind looking at our neighbor's arse for another day.'

I sat down on the couch next to his desk and glanced at our living room. Suddenly it was new, I could see it with her eyes. Lejla's call had turned my life into a museum. I looked at the wall above Michael's computer, at the shelves with his Lego toys, tiny cacti, and books about programming. Across the room a different wall opened out, full of my dictionaries and encyclopedias, with the black-and-white photo of bewildered, gray-haired Salinger with his tight fist ready to smash the vulgar lens. Between our two untranslatable worlds, the round dining table we built together one evening, fighting over the instructions. Next to the big TV, a photograph of his dog. Diabetes, we had to put him to sleep. Michael held Newton by the big black paw, while I held Michael's left hand,

and the dog sank into sleep. Michael was crying, he kept wiping his nose on his shoulder, because he wouldn't let go of Newton and me, the paw and the hand. And then the damn avocado tree, between the TV and the desk, a stubborn plant, a survivor against all odds, small and underdeveloped, without a fruit in sight, yet still alive through the seasons. A slim, desperate tree. I planted it one day, half-jokingly, in a way that was entirely wrong. Later, Michael saw a YouTube video according to which we were supposed to pierce the seed with toothpicks and leave it in a glass of water. I took the seed out of the fruit, wiped its skin, and pushed it deep into the earth like a magic bean. I didn't expect anything; I forgot about it the following moment. To me the whole thing looked like a funeral – the licked, fat seed deep inside the pot. But soon it turned out that the grave was in fact a cunning cradle. It's Michael's fault. Michael watered it, exposed it to sunlight, cleaned the parasites off its leaves. Poor little tree. A zombie avocado. I was sitting there on the couch, staring at it as if seeing it for the first time. Lejla would burst into that wicked laughter of hers if she could see my avocado tree. She would remind me that I'm the kind of person plants go to in order to die, not to live.

I could see her there, on our parquet, glancing condescendingly at my *Dublin phase*. She wouldn't even say anything; she would take Europe off me with her eyes, as if she were taking a fur coat off some new-money tramp, shamelessly revealing my Balkan scars.

Once he stopped typing, Michael looked through the window behind me. Two weeks earlier, a nudist had moved in next door. We could see his dining room from here. He was a middle-aged man, ordinary in every way, with red polka-dot pans and a black briefcase on the chair. One of those who overdo it with the beard in order to restore their dignity after losing their hair. There was a calendar from the nineties on his wall. He ate once a day, right out of the pan. He listened to Shostakovich. Michael was irritated, both by the music and the large crotch that greeted him in the morning.

'Is he home?' I asked.

'No. Thank God.'

I was waiting for him to look at me. He was still staring through the window. Crumbs of potato chips lay in his beard. Had it been a different Michael, the one who existed before Lejla's phone call, the one who cries as he watches a stranger kill his dog, Michael who eats red velvet cake with his fingers, Michael who asks for a bigger screw for the dining-room table . . . Had it been that Michael, perhaps I would have brushed the crumbs off his beard. So naturally that he wouldn't have noticed. But it didn't make any sense this way. Touching a statue in a museum, wiping a speck of dust off David's veins. So I just sat there on the couch, *our* couch, which suddenly became *his* couch, and soon enough just *a* couch, looking at that big redhead god and the coffee stain on his jeans. Would he be able to find the product for difficult stains? His feet, otherwise enormous, seemed so minuscule compared to the sea of wounded parquet surrounding them. Who would get him new slippers? He is never going to think of that. He will walk barefoot, forever, on the lousy parquet floor. I looked at his feet as if they were children I was about to abandon.

'I need to go home,' I said, finally. *Home.* We had lived

together for six years, I shouldn't have said that. Home was our apartment, our books, our bed with anatomic pillows, our broken shower, the duck on the tile in the bathroom, the scars on the floor. Even the naked man in our window. *Home* was not Bosnia. Bosnia is something else. A rusty anchor in a sea full of piss. You keep getting tetanus shots, although it's been years. Bosnia is not home.

'Why do you need to go home?'

I had ready-made answers, grownup answers. I gave him a convincing story about the great opportunity to see my mother, do paperwork, collect old records, a story about a friend from school and her brother who, apparently, lives in Vienna, a story about Vienna which is excellent, perfect, because there's this conference about discourse and power which otherwise I wouldn't be able to attend, a story about cheap flights and how I have always wanted to see Mostar, how the timing was perfect . . . A story about everything and nothing. It seemed, for a moment, that he would understand what was going on, that he would notice the holes in my sloppy code, tell me it was out of the question. I would have called Lejla and explained that I simply couldn't go, Michael was right. I almost hoped it would happen. Like when I get home early and open the door slowly, aware that Michael might be on our couch with another woman. Maybe not even a woman, I think as I quietly lower the handle, perhaps he is just watching porn with some questionable fetish – a large woman defecating on a tied-up man, something like that – and I would catch him. There was always that possibility – that I was right, that I would suffer because of him, that he would manage to hurt me, but I would be right and that would comfort me. Then I enter the apartment, year after year, and find him typing code on the dirty keyboard full of cookie crumbs. The possibilities die out. And now? He will say something. He is looking through the window at where the naked man lives. He is frowning. I will remember this moment for a long time, I thought. And then, one day, I will simply forget it. He just nodded, still looking through the window, and said, 'Sure, whatever you need.'

I don't need Lejla. She needs *me*. It has always been that way. I wanted to tell him that. And about Armin. And about those dogs. Instead, I just said, 'You need new slippers.'

He smiled, replied, 'First the curtain,' and went back to programming. The avocado tree kept growing, silent and still. Its stubborn life embarrassed me.

[You're seventeen. I'm a year older. We're singing '*Gaudea-mus igitur*'. You sing *humus* when it should be *sumus*. I pinch you. 'It's *sumus* first!' I whisper. But you just shout on, proud of being so majestically tone-deaf, even though our music teacher commanded you to lip-sync only.

Our principal is delivering the same speech as the previous year and the one before that. Ever since the peace agreement was signed, he seems to have discovered a new vocation – the underestimated academic who would have ended up who knows where and collected who knows what awards, had history not cheated him. This way, however, the only thing left for him to do is to – modestly, as every true genius must – provide counsel to us, the confused youth.

'You are,' he says with his quivering voice of unfulfilled potential, 'a generation standing before a sea of possibil-ities.' *Asphalt*, an older you would have corrected him. But what did we know back then? You, with your thick hairband on top of your head, in a denim jacket one size too big, and glitter on your cheeks, the stuff you got free with the winter issue of *Teen* magazine. Me, in one of my ragged shirtdresses,

in platform sneakers and with pearls in my ears. We had
no idea what we were singing. Our voices crept out of our
lungs like innocent bats. 'Death will come soon and cruelly
overtake us,' dead Romans sang through us. We will be deep
underground, they said, and no one would save us. Someone
should have translated that bunch of drunken clichés. Or
perhaps it is supposed to be that way – first you sing about
death in a language you don't understand. Later, when you
discover the real nature of the verses you sang in front of
your proud parents, it is too late to change your mind. Your
parents don't understand Latin either. Now you have to
live, live and rejoice, regardless of death. And so the two of
us stand and sing of death, of joy, looking at an undefined
space beyond our parents and teachers, at something as
distant and irrevocable as Latin, lost in the peeling paint on
the wall behind the audience. We are looking at the *sea of
possibilities*. And they are looking back – suddenly proud and
present – as if our yelling woke them up from deep slumber,
from a darkness they had woven themselves only a couple of
years ago. We sing to the sea they stole from us, one glassful
at a time, while we were busy collecting napkins, marbles,
and *My So-Called Life* posters. My mother, quiet and wide like
a lake in her light-blue special-occasions dress, is sitting next
to my father. He forgot to take off his crumpled hat in front
of my whole class. And his walking stick, oak, at my prom,
like a baby brother I never wanted, leaning against the chair
between my parents. Dad nods his head every once in a while,
looks around and whispers something to Mom. I can't hear
him from the stage, but I can guess every word. *That's Kostić
over there, his kid's a moron, it's a wonder he's graduating. And*

there's Lalić and the wife. Their daughter's in Sara's class. Mom is nodding with her eyelids. She is wearing that slimming slip again, you can tell by her cheeks. Unless the whole parade is over soon, she will burn up.

Your mother is sitting alone, not far from them, dressed all in black. Among all those brightly colored blouses, she looks like a punctuation mark. Her collar is crooked on one side; she forgot to pull it out. Later, before the photos are taken, you will correct that silent accident without a word. You will approach her, put your arm around her waist, and lean your head on her motionless shoulder, as if you were taking a picture with a tree. Spring is almost over, but still heavy in all the limp lindens and lily-of-the-valley bells. The sweetened smell cuts through cigarette smoke and proud mothers' perfumes. I am leaning against a streetlight, looking at your mother who hands you some money and tells you things I cannot make out. As if she were buying potatoes. You can't stand her black clothes, but it's prom night, she is giving you money, behind you the church is shining like a freshly polished coffee grinder – there is no point in criticizing her.

After she has gone far enough down the alley, I join you and show you the bills in my bag.

'Fifty,' you say. 'Nice . . . Only twenty here.'

'Just enough. Did you bring . . .'

'Yep. They smell like strawberries.'

'You didn't smell them, did you?'

'No, you idiot. It says so on the package.'

Our refusal to dress up was just as elaborate as the layers of tulle wrapped around our classmates. Mom did all she could not to look at me; she was wearing her best dress, the one she could still fit into, and my skinny legs annoyed her. The police chief's daughter graduated in sneakers and leggings.

The day before prom she took me to buy a bra. I didn't feel like it, but it obviously meant something to her, so I played along. I guess that was her way of getting closer, somewhere where Dad wasn't always going to take my side. She was ready to perform a mother's sacred duty – teach me how to try on a bra *the proper way*. In the changing room, she looked at my ribs, my undeveloped chest, and the sunken stomach with defeat. She grabbed her heavy breasts proudly and said, 'I got these in elementary school. I guess you take after your dad in this too.' My mom, like an insulted teenage girl who needs that one victory, standing before my half-naked body, holding her boobs.

The morning before prom Dad gave me a golden necklace with a pendant the size of a matchbox on which someone had carved my name, surname, and the date in italics. He was staring at the ground, something he always did when he thought he would cry. He said, 'Well done, kid.'

Five or six years later I will deposit that necklace on the sweaty palm of a Dublin pawnbroker. The money will help me get through one month. I won't even have enough for dial-up; I will call my mom from an Internet café. She will shout, thinking the connection is better that way, and Dad will stay silent; instead of him I will hear the voice of an annoyed sports commentator.

Then I will pawn the pearl earrings, Grandma's ring, and two leather purses. I will swap Bosnia for money, so I don't have to go back to it. But on that day I don't know it – in my platform shoes and my hair down to my butt. We have graduated from high school. I'm standing next to you, singing, with the necklace under my shirt so my friends wouldn't see it.

I don't know that one day, with my first paycheck, I will come back to the pawnshop and realize it is too late. I don't know I will be sorry, although the necklace was hideous, and the pendant over the top in every way.

And those two boys we had chosen for the job? It must have been your idea. It was all the same to me, after Aleksandar. I just wanted to get it over with. So I left it to you to organize the whole endeavor as if my virginity was a bank account and you a crafty accountant. You never found it difficult to attract men's attention. In you, they could see what I saw too: the promise of a quiet wilderness waiting behind a damp tree stump deep in the woods. Your eyes were darker than ever, framed with a thick layer of mascara you would forget to take off before bed. You would show up for classes with uncombed hair, in big wrinkly shirts. Before the first teacher got in, I would lick my index finger and wipe dark stains from beneath your eyes. And you looked at me as if you didn't care, with or without the smudges.

I would get liquid foundation out of my bag and apply it over your red nose. I could have drawn a geisha's face over yours – you wouldn't have cared. They could feel it, those impatient boys, full of pheromones like heavy beehives, caught in the middle of a tedious metamorphosis that they themselves had trouble understanding. They could sense your untamable recklessness; it cut to the very core of their wet, unrealized dreams.

I remember the day we had that math test, you finished first – though you had to do both yours and mine – and were staring through the window at the place where the school gate opened to the road. I remember that moment because I caught the teacher looking at your face while the rest of the class were busy struggling with difficult arithmetic. He observed you with a calm, secure gaze, like he could understand something that would remain ungraspable to us kids for at least another couple of years. With his eyes he turned you into a complicated mythical creature only an adult can read. But you just rested your eyes on the gate where, if you looked long enough, a dark-haired figure in a long coat might appear.

Do you remember our scrawny dates? After all the prom rituals were over, we took them to the river, under the great willow. Their fathers' colorful ties were choking their necks. Yours (or was it mine?) brought along a big wooden flask of *šljivovica* with the irritated face of St. Vasilije Ostroški engraved on it. We bought four rows of *sirnica* and a liter of Fanta, to help swallow the *rakija*. The metallic smell of stale spring bounced off the river's surface.

'Have you chosen your major?' my guy asks while I'm lying on the grass and looking at the blurry sky, worried that rain would spoil our plans.

'Literature,' I say and reach for the flask.

'Serbian?'

'And which other?' your guy asks.

Then he turns to you, who are lying with your arms and legs spread open, as if someone crucified you on the damp ground, and trying to whistle. 'What are you gonna study?'

'Nothing,' you answer and go on with your failed attempts to produce more than two tones. The air leaves your lungs in vain.

'You can't whistle,' I shout, trying to change the subject. I have spent the last year of high school begging you to go to college, to which you first responded with a simple 'I need money,' without ever clarifying what exactly you needed it for, and later just stopped answering altogether, but rather changed the topic or just ignored me.

'Surely you're gonna go to college?' your guy asks.

'Why would I?'

'And what would you wanna do? Clean someone's house?'

He says it with disgust, as if cleaning were just as repulsive as soiling. You sit up, leaning on your elbows, and look at him as if he were the dumbest person in the world.

'What's Sara gonna study?' you ask, though you know my choice very well.

I'm quiet, worried that your rude behavior will distract them from their original purpose. We didn't come to the river to discuss your failed future. You don't go to the river for that. It isn't fair to ruin this for me just so you can show some men how unusual you are, so much more unusual than dumb me who wants to study.

'Well, Sara's gonna study literature,' they answer in unison.

'OK,' you say. 'Then I'll do literature, too. Everything OK now?'

You laid your messy head back on the wet ground, closed your eyes, and went on trying to whistle. Your date put his hand on your knee without disrupting your melody. My guy followed his friend's every step since he had no idea what he was doing. A palm on your neck – a palm on my neck. Fingers in your hair – fingers in my hair. That way I could feel everything you felt. My romantic evening was but a poor version of the bad teen movie playing before my eyes, with you in the lead role. My *special night* was just a copy of yours.

Soon we split up, each couple on their own side of the thick tree. Mine had no example to follow anymore and barely knew what to do. I helped him with the condom. The first time I felt him in my fist, it felt like I had grabbed a scared little bird by the neck. I spread my legs and looked at the huge moon. It was hanging in the dead heavens like an undeserved badge, old and mutilated. Its wrinkled lips tried to tell me something, something important. And then, all of a sudden and without warning, the moon got unhooked from the black sky and plunged heavily into the cold river. Water drops sprayed all the way to my bare feet. A perfect silence reigned, darkness was complete. The pain broke through me sharply and unannounced. It took its revenge as if a long time ago, somewhere deep inside my body, I had taken its throne.

The night before, we had cooked a thick mass of lemonade with sugar and applied it to our ticklish crotches. You ripped out my hair, I ripped out yours. I knew it would sting, but didn't complain. I trusted you. Afterwards, I could hear you on the other side of the willow. You were hurting, so I tried to outdo your pain with my own scream.

When it was all over, we remained lying next to our

respective men in their colorful ties, on the ground that smelled of strawberries and Fanta. One of them said it was getting late – we should get going if we still wanted to make it to the hotel party. But you just started singing '*Gaudeamus igitur*' from your side of the tree, and I started laughing and shouting back, 'Not *humus*! *Sumus*!'

We woke up alone at dawn, curled up next to each other as if an invisible umbilical cord from the nearby river nurtured us. At first I didn't know where I was, I heard water hitting the rocks and thought it would swallow me whole and take me far away. Then I saw your black hair on the palm of my hand and remembered that we had lost our virginity just a few hours ago. I brushed a tiny red ant off your shoulder. It still hurt between my legs, but I didn't want to admit it. Besides, I wanted to wake up next to him, not you, but I didn't tell you that, either. Yet you were cruelly unchanged, as if there was no reason to be sad about the whole thing. Everything had gone as you had planned.

We took clean underwear, a pack of aspirin, and the remaining money out of my bag.

'Are you going home right away?' you asked me, counting the bills and the coins.

'I don't know . . . What time is it anyway?'

You glanced at your yellow rubber watch and said, 'Six and . . . Something. What's the difference, it's prom, nobody will mind.'

'And where would we go this early?' I asked, trying to put my crumpled shirt, filthy with grass, earth, and blood, back over my head.

'To the market,' you answered, like it was the most natural thing in the world.

'The market? Now?'

'Yeah, they open in half an hour.'

You were ready in less than a minute, with the black ponytail high on the head and shoelaces in safe, double bows. I was still trying to locate my leggings in the bushes. I went carefully down to the river where my right sneaker lay under the weeping willow's branch. While I was putting my shoes on, I spotted something white among the leaves. It was a kid's glove, with its fingers dirty and ripped. Someone must have dropped it from the bridge, back in winter.

'Look,' I said and showed it to you.

'What d'you need that for? It's summer,' you said unmoved, applying a new layer of glitter on your lips and cheeks. Suddenly you rendered me a child, someone minuscule and defective, a person whose miserable fingers could fit into the tiny glove.

'It's not summer yet, smartass,' I shouted back at you, but you just shrugged, as if seasons were a matter of personal choice, not scientific agreement. It wasn't even seven a.m., and you were already irritating me. My discovery meant nothing to you, just like the hymen you shattered the night before – you discarded both of them as boring and impractical. *What d'you need that for? It's summer.* I wanted to show you that the stupid glove meant nothing to me either, so I threw it into the river with all the force I could summon. I thought the water would soak it and drown it, but it was too small for that. It only slapped on the surface like a leaf and surrendered to the current.

'Why are you going to the market this early?' I asked, trying to climb back to where you were.

'I'm going,' you said, 'to buy a white rabbit.'

You were standing above me, strong and secure like a cross, surrounded by beaten earth and used condoms. Their strawberry scent had long vanished. And there was something foreign in your face, something I hadn't seen before, and I remember what I thought in that moment – I, clumsy and small in my one sneaker. I thought that last night, under that tadpole, you had discovered something I had missed. I thought, in fear, how I would always be lagging behind you in search of some sort of grownup, intangible knowledge, while you were already disappearing into the distance.

I thought that you were gone, that someone had stuffed you with helium while I wasn't looking, and you stole out of my hand like a balloon towards an open sky.]

three

The sky is clear over Zagreb. We have some minutes left before landing. Through the airplane window I can see some water, but I don't know its name. I see nameless streets too, and small houses scattered around like forgotten toys. Vehicles are slow far beneath us, creeping along roads like malicious blood clots through old veins.

I could pick out the Balkans through that little oval window from among any number of views. I don't know much about geography; I don't know what mountains and rivers are called. That might be embarrassing. For me, the Balkans are a color, not a name. Names are easy to forget, you just have to stuff yourself with foreign words, foreign maps, and letters will disappear like sugar on the tongue. But colors remain, like smudges under eyelids, although I had abandoned sentimentalism in my mother's house a long time ago. Colors can't be washed out with kilometers. A heavy shade of green, like forgotten peppers, all dry and wrinkled, can't feed anyone anymore. A sad brown that goes on meandering like a dead river after an apocalypse. The color of a mummy devoured by worms. Visible traces of bootprints, though it's impossible to see them from this height, it's only an illusion. Hundreds of boots over the beaten earth. And shrubs, pale green tumors by the river, tired shrubs, yet still wild. Each one bears a question mark above. Did someone die here? Did someone kill here?

A red-haired boy is sitting next to me, reading a comic book in German. Someone drew a frightened woman in a tight dress over one half of the page; her eyelids are closed with a movement of a pencil. There is nothing underneath them. The artist doesn't have to draw eyes in order to close them, just the lids. The boy's mother leans towards me and pulls the seat belt between our two seats in order to fasten it across her son. The plane begins to shake and the boy grabs onto his mother's hands as if they are stronger than turbulence, stronger than gravity itself should we plunge toward death.

'Primates don't fly,' a long-gone Lejla tells me, freshman year of college, too proud to admit her fear of flying. She never got on a plane. Once I asked her how she was going to see the States or Australia, and her answer was, 'America is bloodier than we are and Australia is full of jumping spiders. Why would anyone want to go there?' But it was all bullshit – she was hiding her fear of airplanes. Although, knowing Lejla, I'm sure it wasn't death itself that frightened her, but the loss of solid ground instead.

The airport sign reads *Welcome to Europe*, in case someone forgot, including those of us who have just flown in from Germany. As we are waiting for our luggage to appear on the belt, the busy staff of Zagreb Pleso Airport run around, so important with their two-minute tasks, straight and firm in their ironed uniforms, as warning signs to a simpleminded peasant that *this* is *not* the Balkans. Soon I find my bag and get a cab.

'Where's the hotel,' the driver asks me.

'No hotel,' I say with a smile, 'to the bus station.'

He shrugs and presses the button on the meter above a pale Mother of God. I should have said *kolodvor*, the more Croatian word for *station*, I berate myself while fastening the seat belt.

'You don't really need the seat belt in the back,' he tells me kindly. He's right. This isn't Dublin.

'Force of habit,' I say.

Two tiny blue eyes observe me from the rearview mirror, cheeks bulging out in a smile. And as we continue the conversation – where I'm from, what do I do, whether I know there's been an accident on the way to Gradiška – a fish truck turned over – I realize where I am and where I'm not. Dublin, Michael, avocado, our naked neighbor –they seem like a play I saw long ago. I'm sitting in a taxi in Zagreb, a man who believes in the Immaculate Conception is driving me to the bus station, I will get a coach to Mostar and – that's it. Perhaps something happens: perhaps they tell me the tickets are sold out, perhaps the bus tips over like that fish truck, perhaps I get lost in Mostar, regardless of all her instructions and apps on my phone. Perhaps I find her and realize it wasn't really her – some other Lejla called me five days ago, hadn't it been a foreign voice, unrecognizable, there's been a mistake. How surprised she will be, that unknown woman, when I appear at the restaurant as someone else, someone she isn't expecting. We will laugh at life coincidences and later, again, each one back to her own thing. Who knows, perhaps we become friends, the wrong Lejla and I. Perhaps there is still a chance that all this is just a mistake. A wrong number in the code on some screen. I will go home before my avocado tree dies.

'Here's the station,' the driver tells me and stops the meter. I thought of all the taxi drivers who, one way or another, have changed my life, unaware of their colossal roles. All those nameless one-time characters that push the story forward with a crafty movement of their two arms, like two hands of an unstoppable clock. I read his name on the license; I want to remember him, though I realize I would forget him the very next moment. I want to give some significance to the man who drove me to the bus station. Cozy in his ignorance, he brought me closer to Lejla. And I even paid him to do it.

After four hours at the station with a liter of coffee, three croissants, and a Croatian tabloid, I get on the bus. I ask the driver what time we arrive in Mostar. Five in the morning. She'll be asleep then. Waitress or not, I doubt she has started waking up before ten. What am I supposed to do in Mostar at five a.m.? Should I wake her up? I've got seven and a half hours to think what to say to her. Unless something happens to the wheels or the brakes. Then I'll be free.

The bus is half-empty, with passengers scattered around the worn-out seats. Some have already fallen asleep, swaddled in jackets too thick for early May. On their faces I can see the kilometers travelled in that same bus, families – sons, daughters, grandchildren – spilled between two countries, and how skillfully they turned about in their seats, as if it were their own living room. Some keep the large cloth bags on the seat next to them, their fingers slipped through the handle. An older man takes his shoes off and, before putting them under his seat, glances at everyone present. Maybe to make sure no one had seen it, or perhaps to calculate which among us might be the thief. There is something recognizable in their faces, in their swollen red joints and sweaty foreheads forever frozen in one worried wrinkle. Over the ragged backs of their seats, short-haired heads of women peep out, freshly dyed before going to Croatia, probably for Easter, and now with limp, greasy hair, ready to be neglected in Bosnia once again. A plump woman leans across the seat next to her and sharply taps the shoulder of another lady who, it seemed, is already asleep.

'Hey . . . You know we gotta get out at the border. Don't get all sleepy now,' the first woman says.

'Oh, let the woman sleep,' a strong male voice behind me shouts. 'We ain't gonna make it to Posušje till four a.m.'

Following this seemingly innocuous debate, all the passengers were now fidgeting. Some addressed the two women who had started the conversation directly, and some, as if to themselves, kept whining over the length of the road ahead of us. Various voices peeped out of the darkness of unidentified seats, some heavy and tired, others squeaky and playful, so that at one point it felt like the bus itself had started talking. I couldn't fall asleep because the most resolute speaker was sitting right behind me, explaining in the small, tight voice of a hungry goose that one time they had to leave the bus in the middle of the night for the passport check, although a pregnant woman was on board and a man with small kids. A lady from the front hooted back that this never happened to her, and she had traveled with her daughter and three grandkids, they were always allowed to stay inside the bus, nobody woke the kids up. A small someone in the seat in front of mine clucked out, 'And where does your daughter live?'

At that point I knew sleeping was off the table. The woman from the end of the bus started reciting the dense branches of her family tree, explaining the unfortunate geography and complicated history with a simple, 'Whatcha gonna do, gotta move.' The barefoot man from the middle woke up to these words, adding, 'Oh, and get my story – daughter up in Germany with her man, the other one studying back in Zagreb, son's got a company in Ljubljana, they make those, what's it called, PVC systems and venetian blinds and what not . . .'

'My sister's in Australia . . .' a hoarse female voice added from the darkness.

'I buried *my* sister last year. Kidneys,' the barefoot man replied in order to seal the contest. Paper beats rock. Rock beats scissors. Grave beats Australia.

The competition continued all the way to Korenica. Some bragged about their buried cousins, others about lost homes. Some had smart children, doctors and engineers, who couldn't find work, others lived on two hundred marks a week after thirty years of honest work. At some point it seemed as if the owl lady won – she had had two tumors removed from her stomach and a couple of years ago the whole uterus, paid the rent with whatever she got selling lottery tickets. Son-in-law dumped the daughter. Checkmate.

I didn't participate in the contest. I had nothing to boast

of. I'm healthy, I come from Ireland, I have Michael, and I'm on my way to Mostar because I've got enough money to support Lejla's whims. It's irrelevant that she ripped a rib out of me with that phone call. How do I compete with their dead, their ruins and miserable pensions? Lejla could do it. She would find the way to put them all to shame and not even feel one bit sorry for herself. I almost wished her there next to me.

We went to the seaside by coach once, freshman year of college. Back when everything was OK. She leaned against the window and stretched her legs over my lap. She whispered, '*At night I listened to the cries of invisible trains.*'

I looked at her in disbelief.

'No way,' I said. I was about to fall asleep. And she just smiled, full of herself and her superiority. The game was to be followed through, no matter the time and place.

I pushed her legs off me and stood up quietly, trying to get the blood to run through my numb thighs again after hours of sitting. The rest of the passengers were sleeping, outside there was only darkness. I slipped through the seats, soundless like a reaper of souls, looking around for any sort of book. Some had their sleeping hands over opened tabloids, others were holding their bags or fans. I found what I was looking for at the other end of the bus, it was peeping out of the backpack of a pimply young man. He was sleeping way too peacefully for someone who had just been reading Kiš.

I went back to my seat, hissed, '*The Attic,*' and then closed my eyes and fell asleep.

My dad told us to sit in the middle of the bus because it was the safest. That's why we sat at the far end, deliberately, to mess with him even though he wouldn't know. There was enough room there for her long legs.

We were going to the island that year. I remembered too the day at the beach when I'd thought she had drowned.

I could almost see her next to me on this new bus that was taking me to Mostar, to an older Lejla. I could hear her shout back a dramatic lie to the sad group in here. 'My mother is blind. She brought us up without eyesight.' She would be capable of saying some silly thing like that just to win a meaningless competition, to be the uncrowned queen of the Zagreb–Mostar route. Not me. I just sat there looking at the black trees through the window. While I was in Dublin, I felt I could run to the end of the city, but some invisible band would stretch and snap me back to Michael, always, like a slingshot, no matter where I'd go. Now it was past midnight, somewhere between Korenica and Udbina, and the band had stretched so far that it had stopped working. I would soon run out of it. It couldn't stretch to Bosnia.

And as the rain started beating down I thought that this was about me too, about Michael and Lejla, about the wheels that would slide and end this story. They took us out of the bus and lined us up in front of the white booth where a heavy orange-lipped policewoman was sitting.

I could see their faces now, all those owls and geese that had sounded for hours in the dark bus; their faces were contracted in a spasm as if they wouldn't get wet that way, their deep wrinkles like riverbeds for melted mascara, their fists deep in broad pockets. One man put a plastic bag over his head. Another tried to light a cigarette, but failed. Once we were back in the bus, there was no more talking. They were silenced by the rain-soaked humiliation. Only a sigh was discernible here and there, like that of a beaten animal that has finally found shelter. The driver turned the radio on, evening news recap. The prime minister of some government, from one side of the river or the other, talked of creating new jobs.

'At least this'll get us dry again,' the barefoot man shouted, which made a couple of soaking-wet passengers giggle. And then it all died out again, the womb of the bus turned into something inert, almost inhuman, like those wet shoes under the fusty seat.

Should I tell these sad people how I left my sloppy god barefoot on the bad parquet in an apartment with no curtains? Should I tell them how I would go back to him, of course I would, why would they even think I wouldn't? Should I tell them how sometimes I imagine that I'm ripping her skin off? She is lying on her couch, which is beige again, and I'm sitting on top of her, tearing her face off in vain. There's always a new one underneath. And she just looks at me, refusing to scream. As if her eyes, mildly surprised, clearly amused by my aggression, were trying to tell me, 'And what did you think, that you and I were cut from the same cloth?'

[Death is gradual at first, then sudden. In the beginning, dogs died one after another. Their lifeless bodies, still warm in winter morning, followed each other irrevocably, expectedly, the way Wednesday inevitably follows Tuesday. We would find them early, before the first News of the day, lying on their sides. A motionless tongue would be escaping from their benign jaws, along with a whole miserable, non-human life. But a life nonetheless.

It started with Mrs. Ristović's dog.

'The tricolor Serbian hunter!' she would shout over the fence.

She would point at the crooked cross sticking out of the small pile of earth in front of her house and scream, 'The tricolor Serbian hunter! The rarest kind! Only jealous pigs could've think of that!'

Back then crosses sprang up and spread like weeds: in backyards, on rearview mirrors, around our chemistry teacher's fat neck, or tattooed like on Mitar's dad's biceps that one time he came to a parents' meeting and everyone listened to him as if he were the president, all because of the tattoo.

Naturally, dogs were Orthodox Christians and were seen off from this world according to custom; so what if Father Ćedo refused to bury Luks, Mrs. Ristović went on, who says that honest folk can't put a cross where they feel like? 'Is it something to be ashamed of? To be a Serbian woman?'

We would walk back from school through her street and hide our giggles each time she shouted 'could've think' instead of 'thought'. But we felt sorry for Luks who, it later turned out, *was* a tricolor hunter and quite rare, though no one had ever seen him hunt. Mr. Mićo, who lived with his two mute daughters in the house with no facade, said that Luks had actually been a *Yugoslav* tricolor hunter to which Mrs. Ristović replied that he and Yugoslavia could go fuck themselves.

'Whatcha think? Those pigs killed him for bein' Yugoslav?' she asked, squinting her eyes and crooking her smile as if suddenly a great Truth had been revealed to her only, a Truth out of reach for us random mortals with no dead dogs and crosses in our backyards.

'Come on, *bona*, don't be ridiculous,' Mr. Mićo would say, slapping the snow off his Lada.

'Me ridiculous? Whatcha think? That it's a coincidence? That scum's gonna poison our food while we're sleepin'. First the Serbian tricolor hunters, then the Serbs. Mark my words,' Mrs. Ristović would say, looking over her fence at us, especially at you and your new sneakers with two-colored laces as if you had strangled the poor dog with them. And Mr. Mićo would give us a conspiratorial wink and go back into his house rubbing his frozen palms.

But soon after Luks, other dogs fell: Mrs. Talić's pug, the

bulldog from that overgrown yard next to the school, my neighbor's ugly greyhound.

In less than a week, there were no dogs left in our block – they were replaced with small, clumsy graves and the sad howling of nobody's cats. Even Mr. Mićo stopped kidding around. Busy with his beloved Lada, he would wave to us without a word as we walked back from school.

We would make our way towards the abandoned juice factory, trudging through heaps of snow on the sidewalk. It was that cruel winter around your eleventh birthday. You got your period and a new name, whereas I, although eight months older, got nothing.

'Does it hurt?' I asked carefully.

You shrugged, as if something like that couldn't be explained to us – dry girls. You were different. There was an untouchable wisdom in your attitude, which dictated that you were the leader and I the follower, like we belonged to different suborders of primates. The blood gave you the power to make all our decisions: where to go, what to do, and how to act. I tried to remind you that *I* was the older one and, there-fore, should be responsible for both of us, but to you blood ranked higher than mere time. And when I said that your new name didn't count because it was fake, you didn't blink. 'Well, yours is fake too,' you said. 'You didn't have it when you were born, you only got it later.'

Until yesterday, you were Lejla, bloodless and clean, like me.

And now this damn Lela sneaked into our friendship, with her menstruation, which she refused to explain to me. I hated her. Your mother took care to remove the letter G from the front door with a kitchen knife and glued an R instead.

It was made of brass, glimmering brand new in your surname, humiliating other letters. You became Lela Berić, just
like that, as if it was OK to do that without asking anyone. I
tried to convince my parents to rename me Janet. I would be
popular at school, like Janet Jackson in that black-and-white
music video when she appears at the glass door and everyone
around her stares in awe. You would die of envy. However, my
mother told me not to be ridiculous, jennet was the Muslim
heaven, did I want to get my bones broken, was I OK in the
head?

'Tell me. Does it hurt a lot?' I insisted.
'Well, it's like . . .' you replied, 'like having a balloon
expanding in your belly.'
'And is there like a lot . . . of that blood?'
'No.'
'Well, how much is there?'
'I don't know, like a glass.'
'Like a glass for juice or a *rakija* glass?'
'Geez, Sara, you're impossible. I don't know. Wanna see it?'
I shook my head as fast as I could. The day before, when
Mitar cut his finger and started crying during math, you told
him he was pathetic because you bled ten times as much and
didn't cry about it. The teacher expelled you from the class-
room. Again. So I knew that you would have been capable of
taking off your leggings and underwear and all, there behind
the juice factory, and showing me your blood. I changed the
subject quickly.
'What did Armin tell you?' I asked.
'Nothing.'

'And did you tell him I didn't get mine yet?'

'Why the hell would I tell him that? What does he care about my friends?'

'Well, just asking . . . But don't tell him.'

'And why would I do that?'

'Doesn't matter. Just don't tell him. OK?'

'OK, Sara . . . Wasn't planning to anyway.'

You wouldn't have understood. He was your brother. Though I was dying to tell you. About what had happened under your cherry tree the day Mr. Radman's setter died. I had come to collect my religion notebook, the one you had used to copy prayers because you had missed classes. Thanks to some magic trick or other, you had managed to avoid religion which we, mere mortals, had to endure twice a week. And then, just as mysteriously and unfairly, you got a new name overnight and the religion teacher said you could join us, as long as you got up to date with the curriculum. I didn't really want you back. It was the only subject I had without you, something that was mine, something about which I knew more than you did, which I could explain to you later. And now that would all be over. Half an hour of copying my prayers and that's it. You would come to class and know everything. In fact, you would know even more, because I had probably missed some details, some hidden meanings, which you had natural sensors for.

'What's a *womb*?' you asked during lunch break, looking at the prayer in my notebook.

'How should I know?'

'Didn't the religion teacher explain it?'

'Nope,' I said. 'Just learn it by heart, and that's it.'

'And this . . .' You turned a couple of pages and read, '*all things visible and invisible.* What's invisible? The air? Organs?'

'If you wanna come to religion class, you're gonna have to cut the dumb questions,' I said and you rolled your eyes. 'And I'm gonna need my notebook before the weekend.'

Naturally this last comment was ignored. And I didn't really need the notebook, you could have given it back in school next week. But I was afraid you would spend too much time reading prayers and would come to religion and be a smartass. So I decided to go to your place, uninvited, and demand my notebook back, cold and proud, like a spiteful martyr.

Your house shared a fence with the biology teacher, who smelled like pear *rakija* and liked to play with your braids. I looked at his little window as I opened your gate, a rusty mechanism I could solve one-handed in the middle of the night. He had once told me, the drunken toad, that I should try to be more like you, after giving me a C in biology. It took ten steps from the gate to your front door, and yet it was enough time for me remind myself of all the reasons I was upset with you: the biology teacher, religion class, my notebook which, in any case, you should have returned to *me*, and the glued shiny R mocking me from the fake surname on your door. All of this made me bang three times with my fist, instead of knocking lightly.

Armin answered the door so quickly that I thought he

must have been standing there the whole time, watching me frown through the peephole. The moment I saw him, I forgot what I was upset about – his presence reminded me why it still made sense to be your friend. I could have come anytime whatsoever, opened the small gate, made those ten steps across the front yard, and knocked, just like now, because after all you and I were best friends.

And he would be there, him and his palms smudged with color, the tip of his left middle finger swollen and black from the thick HB sketching pencil. How amazing that was, back then, that someone should have a brother who lived, walked, ate, and slept in the same place as you did, someone who was neither your parent, nor your friend, who knew you better than anyone else, though he really knew nothing about you.

'Lejla went to her chess group,' he said.

'She's got my religion notebook,' I explained, as seriously as I could.

The house was quiet; your mother had gone to work. Armin and I entered your bedroom together. I had been there so many times before, but without you it looked different. In his presence I felt embarrassed for your mess, as if he would in some way associate it with me, just because we were friends and the same age.

I remember the huge Janet Jackson poster, which would later be replaced by a mirror; I remember the pajama bottoms, turned inside out, exposed on the crumpled sheet like a pervert; I remember a tower of comics teetering dangerously under your desk – we would get rid of those before college for the sake of your mother's mental wellbeing; I remember a chess piece, the knight, on the shelf where a couple of years later Armin's beach photo would stand; I also remember two socks, one checkered, the other white, sitting on your chair defending your throne from any unwanted usurper.

I wanted to get out of there as soon as possible. Armin found my messed-up notebook in the chaos on your desk and handed it to me. In that shirt and those pants he looked like your father – that is, the photo of him that was in the china cabinet. His eyes roved over your room impassively, at times landing on my high ponytail. I wanted to remember him that way – clean and ironed – so that my father's words would flee in shame before all the indisputable evidence.

Dad said that Armin *and that scum gang of his* had probably poisoned our neighbors' dogs. He said that it was a group of boys working together; they had already brought one of them in for drawing graffiti on walls and they wandered around like mad hounds doing God knows what.

'It's Mar-ko Be-rić now, mind you, not Armin anymore,' my mother added, frowning, as if she had never heard the name Marko before. She handed the golden-colored chicken across the table to my father.

'Marko Berić,' my father repeated in disgust and took another oily leg from the bowl. He was nibbling on it, still frowning, and I didn't dare question his words, or ask him why Armin would want to poison someone's dog. I did nothing, Lejla. I kept eating in silence.

'Is that it?' Armin asked me, checking the notebook as if he had never seen such an object before. I should leave now, I thought. But I didn't want to. I liked the way he looked at

me – as if I were sixteen too. And menstruating. A pearl earring lay on your desk next to the small violet lamp with no
bulb. I took the earring and put it in my pocket while Armin
wasn't looking, so automatically and skillfully, as if that had
been the whole purpose of my visit.

'Can I go to your backyard? I think I lost an earring there
under the cherry tree.'

I was already thinking of ways to tell you what happened,
ways to explain your missing earring to you, while remaining
certain that you would figure it all out, that you would read
me like a phone book and wouldn't let me come over anymore. What if you told them – your mom and Armin – how
you couldn't find an earring? What if your brother found out
I was a liar who hadn't even gotten her period?

I walked after him, down the path behind your house, the
earring hot in my sweaty hand, certain I was being watched
by the smelly biology teacher from his little window. He would
see everything, I thought. He would discover my crime, that
disgusting pig.

Armin walked straight and like a grownup, making me
embarrassingly small behind his back. He kept his hands in
his pockets. His hair was just like yours – black, uncombed, as
if someone had left it behind on his head. When we reached
the old cherry tree, he took a box of cigarettes from his pocket
and lit one.

'That's bad for you!' I shouted, regretting it immediately.
How stupid could I be?

'It's bad for little girls to wear their hair in a ponytail.'

'That's not true. You made that up.'

He smiled like he was aware of some obvious joke I had

missed. I tried to understand what was going on. I told a lie and now I was with Armin. *With Armin.* I am in his backyard, your backyard, and we're talking. We're having a *conversation.*

'And anyway, I'm not a little girl.'

And that's when he did it, that thing I have never told you, not even years later when we buried Bunny and nobody remembered that earring anymore. I have never confessed that your brother untied my hair that winter you got your period. He came so close to me that I could see the scar on his cheek. You told me he had got it in a bicycle accident, he had come home covered in blood and your mother had scolded him, how immature he was and how he should be more careful given that he was the only man in the house. I was inappropriately close to that scar now, right above me; I could have reached it with my tongue if I had stood on tiptoe. Never before had I been so close to a man's shirt. It was clean and ironed, smelled like lemons. My father used to wear his police uniform, but wouldn't let us touch him before work – he didn't want to get all crumpled. I could inspect its fibers now, the fibers of *a man's shirt.* It was soft, though I couldn't touch it, soft to the eye. Armin squinted, as if solving a chess problem, held the cigarette with his lips (the smoke was getting into my eyes but I didn't want to close them), and reached for my hairband with both hands. Covering me like a tree, he pulled the bobble and untied my ponytail. He was gentle – like it wasn't the first time he had done it.

My hair tumbled around my face. And I thought to myself that I wasn't twelve, but a hundred and twelve, and that I had spent that whole century waiting for Armin Begić to set my hair free.

He took a couple of steps back and leaned on the tree to take a better look. At that moment, he looked so much like you that it made me feel awkward.

'See. That's better. Like Venus.'

'Like *what?*' I asked. But he just dropped his cigarette, stubbed it with his foot, and looked at the grass.

'Where's that earring of yours?'

I straightened my hair quickly with my sweaty palms, while he was busy looking for my lie among the clover. In all my confusion, I had forgotten about the earring in my pocket. I was about to take it out and throw it in the grass, when I heard your voice behind me.

'Well, look at them!'

I felt like I was naked in your backyard. I turned slowly, trying to brush my messy hair behind my ears, and met your gaze.

You were leaning against the house, with three bananas in your hand, squinting at us with suspicion.

'Like Adam and Eve,' you said.

I stuck my tongue out at you. You both laughed, like you were a hundred years older than me and knew everything there was to know about this world, things I would never learn. And you looked the same: the same crooked smile, low eyebrows, vulture-like shoulders under a sharp, black bush of hair. There was untranslatable wisdom in your black eyes, a knowledge that would always make me seem small and ineffectual. You two were the same, yet you weren't as gentle as he was. You pulled, shoved, hit, and kicked. You bled. Like a smaller, animal version of Armin. I was standing on *your* territory, wrong like a streetlight in the middle of a forest.

I looked up, something fluttered in my peripheral sight. The biology teacher came out onto his balcony to hang his shameful laundry. He was looking straight at me, as if he knew everything.]

four

I can't, not even for the sake of the story, remember how I managed to find the small restaurant where she worked. I only remember how Mostar glimmered, like a polished jug, though the day was inexplicably gloomy, in spite of the unbearable heat. I remember tourists and their synthetic parasols. They spread across the Old Bridge like a wreath of plastic flowers on an important grave.

I saw her before I realized I was looking at her. In front of the low wooden fence, a couple of pink-skinned tourists snapped photos of the hostesses in traditional clothes. One of them pursed her lips and sent a toneless kiss to the fat Austrian's iPhone. The other, her smile automatized for the photo, looked down at two fat cats next to her clog. They were enjoying a discarded rib of a less lucky animal. She stared at them as if envying their being on the ground, with their loose bellies and oily whiskers, completely naked, while she was boiling in her Ottoman noblewoman's costume, borrowed from three separate centuries. The outline of two scrawny legs, like a small ostrich's, was visible under heavy pastel-blue *dimije* with gilded threads hanging undone. A red Wonderbra could be seen under the coarse white cotton shirt – she had forgotten to button her *jećerma*, which would have covered that chronological slip. A braid – bleached white against the violet *katifa* – climbed the velvet material and disappeared under the red fez and its crumpled kerchief. She was standing like that, entranced by those vulgar cats, like some *Cosmopolitan* version of Hana Pehlivana from the old song, without her *feredza* over her to protect her modesty, without her captain, without the verses, as thin waiters dressed as *beys* and merchants jumped around her, with Parisian steaks and fries on their round, engraved trays. That's when I recognized her. Red lips in a crooked smile for the accidental camera; the tiny mole next to the made-up eye; an elbow raised in order to scratch the armpit under sweaty cotton . . . It was her, Lejla, still grand under the exaggerated props, still spiteful and sweaty and of *this* century, regardless of all the previous ones stacked on her shoulders. It was *her*, like that day on the beach. And despite my cheap jeans from Dublin, and my Michael in his diamond-patterned sweater, and the money I had saved in a distant bank, my poetry and prose, despite everything, I was once again ready to be nothing but Kumrija the handmaiden, to pull some ugly imitation *jelek* over my head, tie red silk made in China around my waist, or at least turn into one of those cats at her clogs, just so she would talk to me, fill my ears with us, with what we once had been, under that cherry tree or next to that stinky river. I wanted her to tell me it was over now, it was time to stop pretending, or else she would eat my ribs, one at a time, for all the tourists to see. I pictured my blood on her shirt from a century past. And she just kept staring at those fat cats, that white-haired woman in fake *dimije*.

I sat in a bar across the road from where she was working, and ordered coffee. Grounds of bitter residue collected on the surface of my converted tongue. I had forgotten the taste of our coffee, Bosnian coffee, Turkish coffee, *homemade* coffee – whatever they called it, the taste was the same. I used to drink double espressos in Dublin; there was a distance between the bean and me, a whole machinery whose aim was to kill the memory of the earth in which the coffee had grown. I had known baristas, their sepia certificates set in expensive designer fonts hung from the walls of fashionable coffee shops, all in order to translate the language of raw coffee to my allegedly refined palate. But that *finjan* in Mostar received me the way a proud laundress would receive her promiscuous daughter after a night out – it reminded me where I was from and where my place was. *That* was coffee, not just an expensive postcard from Colombia.

Regardless of all the tourists strolling down the cobbled path, staining ceramic souvenirs with their oily fingers, our language came to me: at times unnatural, out of joint in its softened accent, and at times completely mine, shamefully and irrevocably mine, with swallowed vowels and stretched-out diphthongs. During my *European wanderings* (as Lejla would later mockingly dub them), I would sometimes hear one of our words in the corner of the mall or by the pole of the metro. 'Maybe,' some stranger would say, looking at his opened map, 'are you sure?' or something like that. In those moments of uncomfortable recognition, I would hide behind my huge phone or the newspaper afraid that *our man* would discover me. One look at me and he would know I understood, he would address me, turn me into *our woman* right there in front of everyone. But it was different this time. *Our language* was everywhere, whereas English, French, or German could only slip shyly through the tight passage between our front-palate consonants. I was surrounded by the same words I had cleansed myself of, the way a man who finally quit cigarettes might find himself closed in a smoking room.

Two sugar cubes lay on the little metallic saucer next to the bitter coffee. The sight of them reminded me of my mom, big and quiet as she was, her plump fingers laying the sugar cube on the tongue before filling her mouth with coffee. Sometimes the movement would last – her mouth would stay open as the wobbly hand went on the long journey to the cup and I could see the sugar melting on her dark tongue. I would catch my father looking at her too – what does she need another cube of sugar for, she should watch her weight, all spread out like a wedding tent. I never ate candy when he was around. I was scared that someday he would look at me like that.

Lejla didn't see me. She was standing there at the gate across the street, greeting tourists for hours, luring them into the restaurant with her long menu. Her mouth moved in the names of steaks and soups. She was out of my eyesight just once – I was ready to run across the road to make sure she hadn't escaped – but soon she came back with fixed makeup and without the kerchief over the fez. At the end of her shift, she went inside to change, an opportunity I used to pay for the liter of coffee and three pieces of *sirnica*, which I ordered not out of real hunger, but only to justify my rudely long stay. When she reappeared, she was in pale jeans that were ripped at the knees and a shirt with broad white-and-blue stripes. The braid and the makeup stayed, pink strap-on shoes replaced the nineteenth-century clogs. She still had the habit of twisting her foot while standing and talking to someone – I could see her ankle, bulging out dangerously in the unnatural pose of an injured ballerina. A short form with red hair and crooked teeth had gotten into her wide *dimije*. Lejla said something to her replacement and the girl laughed, showing her unbecoming gums.

I was standing on the other side of the street. I couldn't cross it. Compared to her white hair and long blue nails, I was old and boring in my black jeans and washed-out yellow top. Once, at the beginning of college, she had told me that my effort to look inconspicuous was entirely conspicuous. That was the sort of memory that returned to me then – small and meaningless. The night I stayed over, sometime during high school, because Dad had slapped Mom. I remember how she had once licked my eye in a nightclub because a speck of dust threatened to ruin my makeup. I remembered her black hair floating on the surface of the Adriatic.

I pulled out the handle from my wheeled suitcase and stepped onto the street. At that moment, a shiny black jeep with foreign plates almost put me out of my misery. It stopped right next to me and honked so hard that everything stopped – the waiters froze with their trays, souvenirs stopped clanking, even those cats looked up at me. That's when she saw me. She rolled her eyes and said, 'Geez, you mad woman,' as if we had only parted that morning after breakfast, not twelve years ago. She gave a sign to the angry Danish man to drive on, 'What, are you all frozen up like a statue?' after which everything returned to normal: the waiters, the postcard-sellers, the coffee machine. It all came back to life under that single gesture of Lejla Begić. She crossed the street, stopped in front of me, and checked me out from head to toe – as if someone had sent me from a transport company and she had to make sure I was right.

'Got your license?' she asked. After *go fuck yourself.* After elementary school, high school, college. After the buried Rabbit. After half a life, if not a whole one – whether I had my license.

'Hello, how you doing, what's up, are you OK, how are your folks . . .' I said all this in irritation, although it was clear to me that we had never been ones for idle small talk. She rolled her eyes. Only then, when she looked at me properly, did I realize her eyes were dark blue. She was wearing colored contact lenses.

'What's that in your eyes?' I asked.

'It's Sara.'

'No, for real. What do you need that crap for?'

In third grade, when I appeared at school wearing glasses, she asked me the same thing. I had to explain the laws of myopia to her, who found them completely illogical, given her ability to see all the way to Jupiter's red spot. If I am shortsighted, it must be my own mistake. I must have broken something.

'What do you care what I have in my eyes?' she asked

coldly. 'Do you have a driving license?' she repeated her question.

'I do.'

The end of high school – we got drunk after I passed my driving test first time. I remembered what she had told me that night, 'That's a police daughter for you, and the rest of us mortals gotta go four-five times till they milk us like cows.'

'International license?' she asked.

'Yes. Will miss require anything else? A blood test perhaps?'

She gave me her crooked smile and looked at me again.

'You're skinny,' she said.

'You're skinny, too,' I replied, 'and you have white hair. And blue eyes.'

'And a husband,' she added coldly, then started walking down the street mentioning the vehicle registration and savings in the bank and what not.

I followed her speechlessly, dragging my suitcase through alleys which, who knows when, became hers – she dodged the holes in the crooked sidewalks with the certainty of a local Mostar woman. I trudged behind, tired from the bus and the fake spring day that was all foggy like before winter. I tried my best not to enjoy the fact that we were on our own and that, again, we had a plan.

In front of some building, which at some point had become *her* building, a guy with a red suitcase was waiting, tall and unseemly, with tattooed hearts and ornaments fading on his broad biceps. He was both young and balding, with an early father-wrinkle between his unkempt eyebrows. The husband, I supposed.

'Dino – Sara. Sara – Dino,' Lejla said, as if reading a boring train route. She unhooked the keys from his thick thumb and pressed the button to unlock the car. Amongst all the cars parked in front of the building, a white Astra sang under pressure.

Dino and I stood by the building without a word, not knowing how to act around each other. The only thing connecting us in life was that lanky woman opening the trunk – too little for a relaxed chat, but enough to share the same fear. As if we had done time in the same prison but at different moments. There was no softness in his eyes for *Lejla's childhood friend*, no I-finally-meet-Sara look. I was obviously a nobody to that man. Even worse – a nobody who would take his wife out of the country.

She soon returned to us and pointed with her blue fingernail at the red suitcase in front of her husband's flip-flops.

'Dino, could you . . .'

Before she could finish her sentence, the giant man lifted the luggage and carried it to the trunk where he laid it softly, but seriously, like laying a casket in the ground. I thought of Michael and the photo of his feet he had sent me that morning – he got sunburnt in sandals. I replied with signs, '(: <3 :*'

Dino came back and, without asking, took my bag as well and carried it to the Astra.

'Doesn't fit,' he said, still trying to solve the problem as if it were an obscure arithmetic theorem. He was obviously one of those men who enjoyed that kind of task – arranging bags in the trunk, fixing the sink, changing a bike tire – and approached them with the gravity of a scientist, as if to expose and justify the indisputable purpose of his enormous body.

Lejla went to him and managed to solve the problem of bags in the trunk in a few moves of her thin arms – the horizontal became vertical, the blanket was moved to the backseat, the inflatable lilo was thrown out. She was about to discard a tennis racket as well, but something made her change her mind so she just put it back on the blanket. While she was turning my suitcase I noticed the wedding band on her right hand. It was golden, thick, and too big. If it hadn't been for Lejla's angular joints, it would have slipped off her finger.

The goodbye was long and overdone. I was sitting at the steering wheel and observed them in the rearview mirror. She hung herself around his neck, climbing on tiptoe. He caressed her back, then her ass. She said something. Kissed him. He wiped his eyes – from sweat or tears, I couldn't tell. And that was it. She got into the car and told me to drive, in a voice of a calm paranoiac, as if Dino would realize a horrible truth and stop us unless we left immediately. But I couldn't turn the key in the ignition yet. Something was restless within me, afraid before that long road that awaited us. I turned to her and whispered, although nobody could hear us anyway, 'He's . . . I mean . . . He's fine? There, in Vienna?'

Lejla put her hot palms on my cheeks and smiled just barely. For a second, through the overly made-up face, I could finally trace the little girl who used to do homework with me. As if she couldn't utter his name either, she nodded slowly, and I could feel my chin starting to shake the minute I got her confirmation. I could sense in myself the swelling cry of a newborn filling her lungs with oxygen for the first time.

'And it's really silly to cry while he's waiting for us,' she said gently.

I obeyed without a word, nodded my head quickly, and swallowed the tears. Then I turned the engine on and changed gear. I was ready.

Ten minutes later she was in the backseat, trying to change into a pair of shorts and a tiny T-shirt. Her long legs kicked my seat and the car door; her arms went through the windows, while her head tilted under the roof. The red bra ended on my lap.

'Couldn't you change at home?' I asked her, trying to read the signs to leave Mostar and get rid of her clothes at the same time.

'Dino would never let me leave the house in this.'

'Does he know we're going to Vienna?'

She just shrugged, which I didn't know how to read. A blunt green flashed in the rearview mirror – a huge bruise across her protruding ribs – and then it disappeared again under the T-shirt. I could see fingerprints on her arm as well; someone's big fingers left a cherry trace on Lejla's skin. And her right temple – wasn't it a bit darker than the other one, regardless of all the makeup covering it masterfully? I didn't ask where all the bruises came from. The right to silence was always more important in our friendship than the right to questions. Even twelve years later – when I was no longer sure about the existence of any friendship between us – I still respected that rule.

Once she had changed, she squeezed over the gearstick to the front seat, more naked than dressed. Then she took the wedding band off her right hand and tied it onto the air-freshener ribbon that was hanging from the rearview.

'Someone should write a book about you,' I said and shifted to fourth gear.

'You can do it,' she replied and then added, 'when you grow up.'

[I don't know who told me. It seems now like it has always been that way. There was never a *before* knowing it.

Armin disappeared after all the dogs had died. After untying my hair. After your menstruation. He, you, and I in your backyard, next to the cherry tree, your earring in my pocket. Surrounded with grass, cigarette smoke, and my messy hair, I didn't know I was already standing in a mutilated future memory. I can't remember what I was wearing, what we talked about later, whether I said goodbye before going home. I can't remember because nobody told me to memorize all that. Each time I lose a tiny bit of the picture: the clover disappears, the houses in the background disappear, the laundry on the balcony disappears. Armin is unchanged in the simplified backyard of my crumbling recollection – a sixteen-year-old looking for an imaginary earring among wilted clover. Every memory of him before that event was suddenly poisoned with this new knowledge. Every Armin before – the one from your seventh birthday, the one in your room, the one standing under the cherry tree – became the Armin who would be gone.

I don't know how I found out. It doesn't really matter. I just remember that the town looked different, as if someone had sucked out all of its juices and let it dry out in the grass. There was more and more darkness, more canceled classes, more prayers in the daily papers. There were fewer magazines, less music, and less food. The dark spread around as if some mean kid had spilled it over us. Townspeople suddenly got new faces. Some had frowned just once and stayed that way forever. Others were gone for good, left without much noise. I would lie to foreigners later on. I was too little, I would say, I wasn't even aware of what was going on. But that's not true. We knew, you and I. We knew *it* had started, that they had started it. We knew it would last. Soon it was a constant, like an extra chemical element in the air. It was easy to say its name, roll it over the tongue like *good morning* or *good night*. It was everywhere: in the linden tree behind the school, in kids' drawings in the school toilet, in the teachers who suddenly used the Cyrillic alphabet only. It was in you, in your new name, merged with Armin's disappearance.

You spent more time at home, confined by your mother's concrete fear. One morning you found feces on your doorstep. Human, in a pile. You told me you had never seen so much shit in one place. 'Someone worked hard.' But you didn't care, you and your mom. Armin had taken fear, embarrassment, and shame away with him. He had turned them into second-rate emotions.

I would come up with excuses to go out. I spent my whole twelfth year wandering around, although my father had forbidden it. Every day, behind the gates of the abandoned juice factory, I would see the ghost of the small three-colored hunter, Luks, roaming in confusion, looking for a bone. He didn't bother me; it was comforting to run into him during my futile searches. He reminded me of what had been before, that *before* really existed.

I was certain I would see Armin somewhere; I would be the one to find him and bring him back to you and your mother. As if he didn't know his way back home on his own, so he needed me to find him. I approached my town like it was a vast metropolis where one could get lost. But I didn't want to admit that our town was too small for such a thing. People couldn't get lost there. They just disappeared.

And another memory – the day I decided to give you back the stolen earring. The last time I had come over, Armin had untied my ponytail under the cherry tree. And now this void. The fence is suddenly a different fence. An immense vacuum gaped behind it. You let me in and told me to take my shoes off. The snow, as always, was dirty and half melted. I obeyed silently and entered the dark corridor. Armin's absence filled the space more than his presence ever had. As if someone had pulled the ceiling down just an inch, and the walls had quietly moved closer to each other during the night.

I noticed there were fewer things in the hall and in the living room: the big needlepoint picture of two deer had disappeared, the long wooden clock had gone from above the TV, and later the TV went as well. You sold everything you had, including those saucers with colorful squares, the ones I used to eat your birthday cakes off. You sold most of your Barbie dolls, except for the black-haired doctor. But you didn't care – Barbie dolls, like emotions, became something insulting.

Your mother wore a black dress when she went downtown

and a black tracksuit when she stayed in. It was pale, this blackness of hers, as if someone had drawn her with a pencil. Perhaps that's why they stopped bothering you – you had enough of that washed-out blackness, it was pointless to add anything to it. But you wore your colorful slacks and red sweaters, like a little chromatic version of your mother. 'Black's when someone dies,' you said, and I agreed quietly. Armin was not dead; he was simply somewhere else, somewhere where it wasn't this dark.

You didn't wear black, but you tidied up your room. Tight bed, with perfect angles. A teddy bear on it. I can see your carpet and the color of your desk for the first time. A tape in the player. Nirvana. That's Armin's music, I wanted to say, but didn't. It belonged to you now; I could see it in your face. Janet Jackson disappeared from the wall. In her place, you hung a big square mirror, which would stay there forever, or at least the *forever* I have access to – Hare's death. He didn't exist back then. He would be born later in your story, conceived by some village whore, and we would see him in Mr. Kraljević's crate on that deflowered morning after prom, but we don't know that yet. I'm standing in your room and I don't know that one day I will see us in that same mirror, sitting on the brown couch and drinking wine after Bunny's funeral. For now we are tiny in it, glittery, me without blood, you without a brother. Our story seems to have finished, though it has only just begun.

No books on your shelf yet, no Crnjanski, that would come later. For now there's only one new photo there. Armin in his swimming trunks, leaning against some kind of rail. A pale photograph – or did that paleness come later? I don't know. I felt your earring in my pocket and remembered why I had come over. I was supposed to give it back, I regretted having taken it in the first place. It was never my plan to steal it, I only wanted an extra minute with Armin. And now he was gone. I didn't know how to return stolen jewelry to someone whose brother had disappeared. I was embarrassed by the smallness of my crime.

I spent that year wandering about the filthy streets with the earring in my fist, waiting to get my period. I was certain I would bleed the minute I found Armin. It made sense back then – I had to wait for his return.

That's how I thought about it then, in that epic and final way twelve-year-olds tend to be. But the blood came along, disappointingly lonely, sticky and painful, in the middle of summer, with a mother too busy with the power cuts to explain it to me. You only said, 'Just some blood,' and shrugged it off. Now that we both had it, it was no longer special. Things retained their supernatural essence only if they happened to one of us. Then the other one could daydream about the missing thing. Now we had to wait for the next difference to bring us close and force us apart at the same time. But you still took care of me while my big mother kept herself busy reorganizing her better-life magazines. You told me to chew parsley when it hurt; to warm some rags up by the stove and wear them on my lower back, under my shirt; to strain on the toilet to get as much of it out. You said pain was good, the problem is when it doesn't hurt and the blood surprises you.

'It's not just blood,' I told you in the schoolyard. 'It's not completely liquid. Something else comes out, like gooey . . .'

'Well, yeah . . .'

'*Yeah* what?'

'It's the little bits. From you, inside.'

'Bits of what?' I asked.

'Where the baby should be.'

I looked at you in surprise. You and your mother had had the *talk*. Your mother – who wore clogs and *priglavke* to the store, in the middle of spring, with hairy legs and graying hair. *She* talked to you about babies, while mine just refilled the thick pads in the cabinet under the sink where Dad wouldn't look.

My mother – the fattest in the parents–teachers meeting, her ankles swollen over the turquoise strap of the sandals. She didn't sit next to yours, no one did. As if tragedy were lice. She only made spinach pie and told me to take it to *poor Mrs. Berić* even though she knew that surname was a fake. I was embarrassed. I scraped the pie out in the ditch that followed the gates of the demolished mosque, halfway to your place. Cats came out of the bushes, a bunch of skinny, limping, half-blind cats came to eat my mother's goodness. One of them, the largest one, with half a tail and blind in one eye, turned bloodthirstily to my unprotected body. She wanted to kill me, I could see it in her one eye, but she changed her mind at the last minute and went back to the pie scattered on the ground. I nodded my head gratefully and put the empty casserole dish in my backpack without a word. I went towards the river, bravely holding in my tears. I have never told you that, about those cats and that pie. I kept that secret along with all the others that could have hurt you even just a little. I didn't tell you that in PE class Milan Kasapić said that Muslims wiped their asses with their hands. I didn't tell you that you had an open seam on your stockings during the St. Sava celebration at the school. I just suggested we stand in the back row in the choir. I didn't tell you what my father had said that day at the table while we ate chewy duck as if nothing had happened.

'I mean, it's no wonder, the kid was trouble. It was a matter of time before some shit would happen.'

'The Berić kid?' my mother asked, scraping the duck leg. The fat oiled the tiny hairs above her lips.

'Berić. If that one's Berić, I'm Mustafa. His mom stopped by the station again.'

'What does she want now?'

'Asking if we have any news . . . Like we're the fucking news agency.'

'And what did you say?' my mother asked, ripping the flesh off the dead bird.

'The hell should I say? Six months and you close the case. She should be happy he didn't end up like Habdić. Times are rough, people go missing, what does she think? He's the first one? She was all like, "Don't be like that, friend, our daughters go to school together." Can you imagine? That I'd be so unprofessional and put everything on hold to go look for that little piece of shit just because Sara, by sheer coincidence, shares her desk with her daughter?'

'Dear God,' Mom said, between two bites.

'And I said everything I had to say. About the dogs and all. I said it all, in front of the whole station. Šušić was there, Tarabić too. They all heard what I had to say.'

'Really?'

'Really. Man, I couldn't hold back anymore. I said that all

those scumbags that went missing, Habdić, the Šehić kid, all the gang were –' Father put the duck leg up in the air like a judge's gavel – 'prime suspects for the crime against our dogs and that it was a matter of time until someone had enough. Those exact words.'

'What did she say?' Mom asked proudly.

'What was she gonna say, stupid woman, "My Marko would never hurt an animal," calling him Marko like I was born yesterday, like I would *help her* if she called him Marko . . . In the end I told her we'd make a couple more posters, which is neither easy nor cheap these days, but whatever, we'd make a couple so she can put them up wherever she wants. Couldn't get rid of the woman . . .'

They left the picked-clean bones in a flower-patterned bowl Mom used for special occasions. What was it that day? Wedding anniversary? Summer break? I don't know. But that damn bowl was an insult to my untied ponytail.

'You didn't eat a thing,' my mother said with contempt.

'For the better. Sara is a supermodel, she doesn't feel the need to stuff herself,' my father said and winked at me like an accomplice. Mom rolled her eyes in response and started gathering the dishes.

'You gonna help me or is the model too busy?'

Father took his walking cane and limped to the couch. *Lazy leg*, that's what he called it. Or *damn lazy leg* if someone asked why he hadn't been mobilized.

'If it wasn't for this lazy leg, Daddy would teach you how to ride a bike, it's good for staying in shape,' he said the day the school organized a bicycle race. And, 'If it wasn't for this lazy leg, Daddy would take you fishing.' And also, 'If it wasn't for this damn lazy leg, Daddy would wipe them all off the face of the earth.' That other father existed somewhere, with two perfect legs; the one who taught me how to ride a bike and fish, the one who came to school meetings and drove me home after a night out and killed *the bad men*. Maybe someone else would have been the chief of police then, some poor man without an eye, a finger, a kidney. Someone who would have found Armin. Mine was there all along, while other kids' fathers were out there in the dark. Their daughters received aid packages with perfumed napkins from Norway and football cards. My dad was still there, all flabby on the couch with a big mug of green tea in his hand – because that kind was good for your metabolism.

'Daddy would get rid of all that scum,' he would say. 'But Daddy is doing what he can with what he has and where he is. Daddy's doing what he can.'

You and I believed that Armin would come back; we knew he wasn't the one who had poisoned those dogs. We thought people would find the real culprit and return your brother as soon as the truth came out. We were sure about it even when the bruised, bloated body of Ozren Habdić washed up on the riverbank by the psychiatric clinic, along with empty milk bottles and beer cans. There was nothing in the news, though the whole school talked about it. He was found naked, people whispered during lunch break, and without *the thing*. I didn't dare talk about it with you, the story of Ozren's corpse swelled up between us like a tumor. And then one day out of nowhere, during biology class, you scribbled on the page with a dissected frog, *Armin is not in the river, he would have showed up by now. Ozren was an idiot.*

I nodded and that was it. It was pointless to consider that case any longer. Armin was smart. He wasn't in the river.

We were the last two people in the world who believed he would come back. We would walk home by the chestnut trees that had posters of your smiling brother pinned to their bark. *Missing: Marko Berić*, in Cyrillic. One of them someone had defaced with the word *balija* in red marker. But we didn't care. We were not interested in Marko Berić. We knew that Armin was alive. That knowledge connected us much more than a shared desk did, it was important to stay together until the end, until your brother showed up again. If we fought, if we split up, that fragile conviction would come undone too. As if his whole life had been woven into the fabric of our friendship. He was to be found nowhere else but there.]

five

And then silence. Her knotty legs covered with blue-yellowish bruises, dusted with crumbs from the chips she wolfed down in two minutes, without offering me a single one. The shimmering wedding band dancing in the air between our heads. I wanted to do something – hit the brakes and send her through the windshield, or at least park somewhere, take my suitcase, and head down the road on foot. I would have walked to Dubrovnik if necessary, until she swallowed her pride and yelled my name, admitting she needed me. But I didn't do anything. I drove fast, but with care, afraid that something might slow us down, that we would never reach Jablanica, let alone Vienna. That Michael would be barefoot forever.

I don't know the names of trees; I only remember that they were silently observing us as we were running away. The trunks were straight and quiet like they had come to our funeral. I didn't want to stop, although I had to use the restroom. I wanted to say something, but was stuck between two Lejlas – the one I had known my whole life, who once waxed my crotch, and this stranger, with bleached hair and slutty clothes, blowing her gum bubbles and letting them burst over her nose. I can't recall half my childhood, yet I remember the details of her with irritating clarity. Blue bubble gum, watermelon flavor. A scratch on her left knee. Cracks in the red lips. One time she had told me that writers write because they don't have memories of their own, so they make some up. That was before, while Rabbit was alive, and we had just started reading books. But she wasn't right, at least not entirely. Memories might be like a frozen lake to me – blurry and slippery – but every now and then there's a crack in its surface and I can put my hand through it and catch a detail, a recollection in the cold water. But frozen lakes are vicious. Sometimes you catch a fish, other times you fall through and drown. I know from experience that all my memories of her tend towards the latter. That's why I had done my best not to remember for twelve years. And it worked. When it comes to our humanity, it's amazing the low levels to which we can sink when it suits us.

And then I answered the phone and said her name. The coldness of the water was familiar. Three-headed beasts lurked in its depths.

We should have been somewhere in the American Midwest in a polished Buick, or cutting Russia in half on the Trans-Siberian Railway. Then I could have named the trees and the small towns, would have googled them in order to sound smarter than I am. I could have claimed that our story was in fact a damn good road trip, that we'd listened to the masters of the blues, eaten spicy cheeseburgers, and had profound conversations with a bunch of symbolic turns. But the fact is that this was her, Bosnia, and me, and I couldn't name a single tree from the row that observed us. The fact is we exchanged just a couple of necessary sentences all the way to Bugojno – about eating and pissing – our topics never reaching beyond primary biological motives. Another fact is that a road-trip story makes sense only when the travelers, albeit wrongly, believe in reaching the finish line, the journey's end that will solve all problems and end all misery. There's no finish line in Bosnia, all roads seem to be equally languid and pointless; they lead you in circles even when it looks like you're making progress. Driving through Bosnia requires a different dimension: a twisted, cosmic wormhole that doesn't take you to a real, external goal, but into the gloomy, barely traversable depths of your own being.

The heat squeezed into the car like a terminal illness, though the sun had already gone into hiding. My legs were swelling up inside the uncomfortable jeans. I was a fat scone next to her who, dressed in half-garments, was cooling herself with a fan. She smelled like sugar, baked coffee beans, and blood. She tried to find something on the radio, but the choice annoyed her, so she turned it off in the end. I didn't dare ask whether there were any tapes in the car. I couldn't make myself start a conversation. With some people, after a bunch of years and stories have taken place, it's impossible to engage in small talk. I wanted to ask her – I was dying to ask her – why Armin was in Vienna, where he had been all those years, why he hadn't called. Had he really poisoned all those dogs? I was afraid. I didn't have any right to extra questions, that I would scare her off, she would find someone else to take her to her brother whose location would forever remain secret to me. I had to follow her rules in order to reach the answers. Armin was alive and I would see him. I would bring him Lejla, dyed and married, but still Lejla. Her pathetic story would become a thing of the past, something that was never right in the first place. Armin was alive all along. The morning after prom when we got Hare, and the night we buried it. She had collected my sympathy on loan. It was about time that injustice was corrected.

After a while I slowed down so much we were barely moving, certain I was driving towards that goal and that the feel of it on that wound would be even more beautiful the longer I put it off; it would correct her mistakes and my silence even more effectively. The road felt slippery, like ice, and cars kept honking and passing us by, while I toyed with the idea that this was the last favor she could ask on account of her missing brother. At least that's what I wanted to think.

And then that darkness. I hadn't noticed it at first. The sky must have changed its mind at some point and slowly pulled the gauze down over its eyes without anyone noticing, like a tired widow in a crowded church. The digital clock above the steering wheel said 15:02, in the pitch-dark, wrong like colors at a funeral. Was that the life she and her tattooed giant were leading? A life without time? It hadn't crossed anyone's mind to adjust the clock in the car? I was annoyed equally by the fact that she was still so irresponsible, and by the fact that it still bothered me. I assumed I had miscalculated the time I had spent in that restaurant, waiting for her to finish her shift. It must have been afternoon already if it was so dark now.

'What's the time?' I asked her.

'Why, you in a hurry?'

'The time's wrong.'

Lejla stretched over and looked at the clock with the expression of a mother looking under the bed to assure her daughter there are no monsters there.

'What's the big deal? A minute up or down. Don't be obsessive.'

Obsessive. One of her words. Back then, before college started, when I thought I was pregnant. 'Don't be obsessive, Sara.' We're sitting in some *kafana* toilet, waiting for the sign to appear on the stick. No, before that, before the stick, when we were studying for the chemistry test. I was angry because she couldn't sit still and study. 'Don't be obsessive,' she told me. Or perhaps even before, much before? Perhaps to her I had always been obsessive. And then I moved to Dublin, met Michael, and started speaking her language. 'Don't be obsessive,' I'd tell him without blinking, at the same time feeling as if I had stolen something, something I didn't think I needed. I had brought pieces of Lejla on me, tiny insects that had crawled into my bag, my pockets, under my pants, and yet they would hide their real nature before Michael. Our first date: an Icelandic movie we both pretended to have understood. 'So what, you're like an artist or something?' I asked. I twisted my foot on the sidewalk and looked at him condescendingly. And he loved it, the Lejla in me, though he never met her. She got to have him, too.

'Lejla,' I said, trying to gather my patience and remind myself we were both well into our thirties. 'Look through the window.'

'Geez, you're such a weirdo. I thought that Belfast of yours would have fixed you up a bit.'

'Dublin,' I corrected her.

'Dublin. Whatever . . . What am I supposed to look at? There's a cow. Yo, cow, what up?!' she shouted and I did my best not to laugh.

'Never mind the cow, look how dark it is. No way it's three p.m. Gotta be at least seven,' I said and she rolled her eyes.

'What difference does it make whether it's three or seven?'

She was getting irritated too, which wasn't a good sign. Perhaps I should have laughed at the cow thing. I hadn't seen her in twelve years and was still scared of some of her reactions. As if I had recovered from a lethal virus back in childhood and was sensing it again. I couldn't fight back the pathetic fear that she would abandon me, she would realize my true nature and change her mind. That first week of school, I was afraid I would say something stupid and she would sit with someone else. Was it possible that I still hadn't managed to shake off that silly fear after all these years? She would sit with someone else and the story would end there. A whole life would be different. I was still afraid. Even that moment in the car, while she irritated me just as much as all the old-times Lejlas, but at the same time scared me like a complete stranger from whom I didn't know what to expect might. Who was that woman in the car with me? Who was I? Or maybe that was us, the real us, if such a thing exists, those silent creatures from the dark depths, everything else was a puppet show for idiots.

'When's the last time you were in Bosnia?' she asked. Her voice was deeper, as if she had just realized a great truth and was looking for words simple enough to pass it on to me, a dumb kid.

'I don't know . . . I can't remember. A long time ago,' I said. I didn't want to admit that I had counted the years.

'Yeah, but more or less . . .'

'What does that have to do with the clock?'

She took a small Motorola out of her purse. Of course, I thought, she still has a flip phone with huge buttons for retired people. So cool. The rest of us are all idiots with our touchscreen tech.

'Can't remember the last time I saw that phone either,' I said and laughed. She rolled her eyes again. This time it was so obvious that for a moment I felt like a lame dad of some cool teenager.

'You're right. The time's off,' she said frowning.

'Of course I'm right.'

She opened the Motorola and pointed the small green screen at me.

'It's not three yet – 14 and 58.'

I hit the brakes so hard she dropped her phone and started laughing.

'Lejla, stop fucking around. What's the time?'

'What the fuck, Sara? Relax.'

'Lejla. What is the time?'

She checked her makeup in the rearview mirror and said, 'I just remembered our Serbian teacher, the one that made us say *wottiss* instead of *what's*, remember? Wottiss the toyme . . .'

She laughed and started typing a text on her clunky Motorola, as if everything were fine. It crossed my mind that she was crazy, I should have guessed as much back in Dublin when she had called. Lejla is mentally disturbed. And I'm the idiot driving her around in complete darkness.

I unfastened the seat belt and started rummaging through my bag for my phone. My phone was, after all, a *smart* phone. Perhaps everything else was crazy: Lejla, her old-school cell phone, the car, the cows . . . But not my phone. No, that one was from Dublin. I could count on it.

At least that's what I thought until I realized she was right all along.

It was three in the afternoon. Even on my phone. Everything was pitch-black. A car would pass us every now and then, the lights cutting the darkness; someone would honk the horn or curse, and then disappear into the night again.

'*Velkam bek,*' Lejla said, in a softer voice. She realized my terror. Even under the fake blueness of the contact lenses, her eyes were something I could recognize. She gave me that face – the Lejla who had lived in my head, the one I had missed and who would, after all the circus, understand that it was enough now, that I needed her to be normal, attuned to my fears. She must have realized that I was lost for real, I wasn't pretending. I had forgotten everything: her and Armin, Bosnia. The darkness.

'But in Mostar . . .' I said, imploring. A car drove past us and honked a couple of times. The driver gave me the finger.

'The closer you get to the sea, the better,' Lejla said, 'that's why I went there. Heartland's the worst. Blind as a bat.'

Heartland. That word always made me think of the human body.

I thought of the two of us in that car as a white blood cell making its way to the *heartland*, in deep obscurity, unaware of the life powering it. I felt completely lost – the car was stopped in the middle of the road, in the impassable night, in a country that resembled my own as much as a funeral mask resembles a living person.

'Sara,' she said carefully, 'we should move, people are honking.'

'Just a second.'

Though I needed a whole extra life. She leaned forward and kissed my naked shoulder. Ten minutes earlier that would have freaked me out, but now I was paralyzed, as if I had to find the levers somewhere inside me and put them to their right position in order to keep moving. They were rusty after so many years. It wasn't enough to resurrect a language – I needed to find in myself something more profound than mere cognition, something carnal and primitive, an instinct that would allow me to survive the darkness. I used to have it, back when I was wandering around our town as a kid, look-ing for Armin. I had the skin for Bosnia. Now I had to grow it again, let it excrete and harden over my naïve European pores in a few seconds.

Lejla suddenly jumped as if she had remembered some-thing, and started unzipping her shorts. She pressed her back into the seat, pushed her hand deep between her legs, and pulled out a thick, bloody tampon.

'Fuck, Lejla . . . That's gross.'

She rolled the window down and launched the tampon into the night.

'What, you want me to get that shock thing or whatever, and then you gotta bury me somewhere?'

'It's not funny, if you need to use the toilet, we'll pull over someplace. I don't need to look at your used tampons.'

'We can't stop here, can't you see you're in the middle of the highway?' she said. And then, as if suddenly annoyed, added, 'And what difference does it make whether *you* are looking or not? They're here, with or without you. Come on now, start the car.'

'I need a second.'

'She needs a second . . . Geez, you mad woman. Can't you see someone's gonna mow us down here?'

When she saw that I wasn't answering, she added softly, 'OK, let's do this: you get us to Jajce. Yeah? It's super close, you can spit to it. I've got a friend there. We can stay the night, if you're freaking out. And tomorrow we go on. You look exhausted anyway. What d'you think, can we do that?'

I nodded in silence. I was too tired to ask questions or fight. In fact, I was thankful. The disgusting image of her bloody tampon pulled me back to reality. I turned the key and changed gear. She cheered up the minute we started moving down the dark road. She found a fresh tampon in her purse and pushed it in while I was trying to block my peripheral sight.

'We can go see the catacombs,' she said cheerfully, as if talking about lemonade stands.

'Sure.'

I had it coming, I thought, answering calls from unknown numbers. Now I had to shut up and drive whichever way Lejla Begić pointed her finger. A bloody finger.

'And we can visit that Yugoslav Council museum . . . what's the name of that freak show . . . The Antifascist something . . . The AVNOJ Museum! The liberation of Yugoslavia!' she shouted and slapped my leg. 'And the waterfall!'

'Sure,' I said, exhausted. 'Whatever you want.'

There was a trace of her blood on my jeans.

['You cut yourself,' someone tells me. The tip of my finger hurts – that's how the memory begins. The rest is blurry, like after rain. Your seventh birthday. I can't remember the furniture, the couch is there in my recollection, although that's impossible – you got it towards the end of high school. I can't remember some big things, but some details I remember with clarity. It's the first time I'm at your house. It smells like chips and soda. I got you the doctor Barbie doll because it was the only one with black hair, like you.

We all take our shoes off at the front door. Your mother is kissing us all, handing out plastic cups with our names written on them in blue and pink markers. Little saucers with colorful squares. Generous slices of chocolate cake with cherries.

What were we doing at that birthday party? I remember my finger hurting. I didn't want to tell you, didn't want to seem like a whiner. You didn't know I was a crybaby yet; I wanted to keep it that way.

I can't remember what I was wearing, or what I looked like. But I do remember the darkness. Someone tells me I cut

myself. Paper – we're playing a game and I got a paper cut. I
whisper, 'Never mind, doesn't hurt.' But I'm lying. It's dark.
Why is it dark at a birthday party? Why are we whispering?
Yes, I remember. We're playing Ghosts. It's your favorite
game. You're holding a candle under your chin, your eyes are
closed, and you're saying some scripted words, as if you have
known them forever. 'If you're here . . . show yourself . . . If
you're here . . . show yourself . . .'

You're scaring me. I have known you for five months,
we're known as best friends. Everyone has one – so you're
mine. But we're not in the classroom now – we're sitting in
your bedroom with other kids in the pitch dark. Yes, I remember now. I can barely recognize you, your black hair falling
over your eyes. You're seven, but in my memory you look like
your older, grownup self. The skin on your lips is coming off,
you can't stop biting them, and your eyes change color, from
black to blue, and back again. I can't make you younger in my
memories; it's always *you*, all those Lejlas in one.

Everyone's quiet, you're the only one talking. I can't
really remember what you're saying exactly, but I do know
we believe you. After all, nobody would dare tell you that
you don't know what you're doing. You're our queen of
darkness, the only one capable of talking to ghosts, ready to
sacrifice us.

You had told us there was a spirit from some past century
living in your house. That only you could talk to him. One of
the boys said, 'As if,' and you looked at him so sharply that he
shut his mouth at once. I was sitting in the corner next to my
saucer with a piece of cake on it, afraid that someone would
take it from me and eat it. My mom didn't know how to bake,

and Dad used to say it wasn't healthy to eat all that sugar. This was a unique opportunity to stuff myself with chocolate.

I pierce the soft cake with a fork and take the cherry with my fingers. It's dark, no one can see me; I can eat as much as I want. And then someone asks, 'Does it hurt?'

'It stings a bit,' I admit in a whisper. I can't see his face. Your older brother. He never goes out during lunch break, always sits in the classroom with those weird friends. And his eyes are too big for a boy. His hair is too long. He reads books that are not for school as if he has nothing better to do with his time. Here, in the dark, he looks like you. Or maybe you look like him? And then, as if it is completely normal to do such a thing, he reaches for my hand. I leave the fork on the empty saucer and let him examine the cut. He's inspecting my finger like a broken toy. His hand is bigger than mine; the skin on his palm is smooth and tight, like I'm touching a balloon. I would retell myself that event later on, once I became a teenager and the sentence *Armin took my hand* started getting new meanings which back then, on your seventh birthday, it didn't have. At that point it's only weird, nothing else. He's older, he knows about these things.

Everything smells like chocolate, cherries, and soda. There's no music because your mother won't let us play any. You explained that this was because you didn't have a dad. He was missing something on the inside, something important. You would finally tell me once we were in high school. He wasn't missing anything; he had a tumor the size of a tennis ball in his throat. On your seventh birthday I don't know what a tumor is yet, I only know you don't have a dad and that's why there's no music. His photo is in the living-room cabinet with the porcelain: your father, in a suit, with a bow tie, singing in Banski Dvor. His mouth is gaping in mute song. Framed LP records on the wall: *Best Ballads*, *Chansons*, and *Town Pearls*. I had heard his name for the first time in our music class. The teacher looked at you after you had sung your two-note scale. She was utterly disappointed. 'Adnan Begić's daughter . . . Who would have thought,' she commented sadly and then quickly added, 'Doesn't matter. Everyone has a talent, we can't all be the same!' But there's no music at your birthday party. As if that gaping mouth from the photo had sucked in all the melody, including your own.

Your brother is still holding my finger in his hand, like he forgot to give it back. He asks what my name is. He asks how old I am. Seven, I say, and add, 'eight in four months,' so he will know I'm older than everyone else in the room. Except for him – he's twelve. I know because you told me at school. He asks when I was born. I tell him.

'Tito died on that same day,' he whispers.

'Who's Tito?'

'Doesn't matter.'

But I won't forget that someone died when I was born, that people can stop and others can start on the same day, same year. I became aware of the cruel democracy of a moment. I won't be able to sleep that night, I will cry because people die, because I will stop one day too, I won't be there. I will wake my parents up; Dad will come to my room first.

'Honey, that won't happen for a long, long time.'

Mom will show up at the door a bit later, annoyed because we woke her up.

'Here, ask Mommy. Folks die when they're very, very, very old.'

And she just said, 'You never know. Gotta be careful,' and scratched her head between two rollers under a headscarf. She went back to sleep without touching me.

But at your seventh birthday party, while Armin is holding my finger, I'm not afraid of death. Perhaps because of the way he said it, *Tito died on that day.* Like it was the most normal thing in the world – to die.

He asks what my favorite color is, out of the blue. I say green, though it isn't really. He asks for my favorite shape. I have to think. I feel the saucer on my lap and say circle.

'That's a good shape,' he tells me, and I'm suddenly proud. My shape is a good shape, not a bad one. I didn't know there were bad ones too. In fact, a few seconds ago I didn't even know I had *my shape.*

He asks a bunch of questions, more than the teacher asked the whole year. But not stupid questions, hard questions – no, he asks me about *me.* What my favorite season is, what my favorite animal is, my favorite number. I have to start my brain, activate it like a sleeping carousel.

'Spring,' I say. And elephant. And the number five.

You open an eye at one point and look at us scornfully.

'The spirits demand perfect silence!' you shout and then close your eye again. I can feel your brother laughing by my side. At you. Without fear. I look at you in panic; I don't want to make you mad. But you're back in a trance, you're talking to some ghost; you took Dejan's hand and now you're shaking it. Nobody is breathing. Every now and then there's the sound of little forks clinking against the saucers. Dejan looks like he's about to faint.

'He's here,' you tell us, 'the spirit is among us.' And then you add in a deep voice, 'Who . . . are . . . you?'

Your head drops as if Lejla has abandoned your body; someone else has taken over your face and is now looking at us through your eyes. Kristina isn't blinking. Dejan is on the verge of crying. Mitar is looking at everyone else since he's not entirely sure what's going on. But I'm no longer amused; you have lost your powers. Armin is asking me questions. I want to live up to the task.

'What's your favorite book?' he asks.

I'm embarrassed – I don't have a favorite book. I don't read books.

'What's yours?'

'*Treasure Island*,' he says immediately. At that moment, it sounds like the best book in the world. I can see the island and the treasure and him finding it.

'Oh, right . . . Yeah, it's OK,' I say coldly and fill my mouth with cake, afraid he would ask something else and realize I have never even heard of that book, let alone read it.

I will ask my parents for it later. Mom will tell me to go to the library and ask for it there. Books are in libraries, where did I think we lived? But I find it. *Treasure Island*, R. L. Stevenson. A blue book with a pirate illustration on the cover. When I open it, there is a card with names. I read *Armin Begić* four times in a row, next to four different dates. I read it every day, the way he would, imaging him turning the pages, worrying and rejoicing, facing the same dangers as me and Jim. I finish it quickly, in case he asks me about it someday. I read it three times, or four. I see it in the college library while looking for *Tristram Shandy*. I touch its spine with my fingers, but don't pull it out. I see it among Michael's books, in English, amongst those computer manuals. I see it so many times, in so many different places, but I never buy it – the favorite book of the twelve-year-old Armin.

He doesn't know that in that moment, while we're sitting on the floor in the dark with my bloody seven-year-old finger. I don't know it either. I'm afraid he will ask me about the book, but he just goes on with his random questions. Do I have a pet? Do I have brothers and sisters? I don't, I have nothing, I have no one. Would I like to have one? Yes: a cat, a dog, a canary, a brother, and a sister.

'The cat would eat the canary,' he whispers.

'No, it wouldn't. The canary would be high up in its cage.'

'What if the cat jumps?'

'I'll punish her. I won't feed her.'

'Then she'll be hungry and she'll eat the canary anyway,' he says and I let out a laugh.

'The spirits demand perfect silence!' you shout from the dark, behind all that black hair falling over your face.

Armin resumes the questioning. What's my favorite classroom – we only have one. What's my favorite tree? What's my favorite flower? I can't tell trees apart, I know about three flowers in total. But I invent, I strain my brain and lie, only to have an answer, to have my favorite. I say the pine tree. I say dandelion. And after who knows how many questions, about my favorite car, song, house, game, cartoon, breakfast, after all my answers, invented, fake, whispered – I feel like I finally exist. I'm a person. Someone with a favorite book and a favorite tree. A favorite shape, which is good, not bad. All those answers filled me like an empty house in a coloring book.

Your mother turns the light on and breaks the spell. Children's hands drop one another, cutting the ritual circle. The spirit leaves you stealthily and disappears through the ceiling. You are Lejla again.

'You know I don't like that game,' your mom says.

'What does it matter, we're only playing . . .'

You answered just like that, with those words, to your mother. Mine would have slapped me hard if I had ever talked that way to her in front of other kids. But yours just said, 'At least let the spirits be, if you won't let me.'

I have never forgotten that sentence. You rolled your eyes and stood up. That's when I realized that Armin had disappeared; he was no longer sitting next to me. He must have sneaked out while you were fighting with your mom and I was staring at you in awe. I didn't like that he'd left, just like that, with all my answers. Where would he take them, what would he do to them? I would later realize that he had only given me one answer – about the favorite book. I felt tricked; it wasn't fair. Even if I had tried, there was no time to find anything out – he was questioning me so fast, like a policeman. So I decided to find out enough about Armin through you, in order to restore some kind of balance and learn to accept that I had given him all my answers.

'What's your favorite color?' I asked you.

'Red.'

'And your mom's?'

'Purple.'

Then I got my courage up and, pretending I wasn't really interested, added, 'What about your brother?' And you never suspected a thing, you simply answered, 'Red, too.'

And so it went on endlessly, because it would have been embarrassing to ask about him only. I remember you had a ready answer to each question. You knew your favorite flower was the poppy, your favorite house was Mrs. Popović's, and your favorite game was Ghosts. And you didn't lie, you knew all about yourself, just like that, instantly. I remember how everything was pretty much the same for you and your brother, so much so that I thought you were copying him. I told you Tito had died on the day I was born, as if to show you that I was special too; I had my own thing.

But you just shrugged, as if the information wasn't worth noticing.

'And do you even know who Tito is?' I asked proudly, though I had no idea myself.

'I do,' you said, 'Mom has a picture of him.'

I spent half of elementary school thinking you were related to him.

I went to all your birthday parties, but I never saw Armin there again. He was growing up, changing; his friends became more interesting than his younger sister's get-togethers. And every time I rang your doorbell, in some carefully selected outfit, with an artfully wrapped present in my hands, I thought that maybe he would be there. Even later, when we were teenagers, alone in your room, years after he had gone missing. I had a favorite band, favorite sneakers, favorite language, favorite magazine. I was ready, in case he came back. And I remember that I always liked to ask you those tiring questions: about your favorite song, your favorite line – because I was sure the hidden link between the two of you was still intact, that everything was the same and I would learn something about him through you, although he was no longer there.

Later on I went to college and, perhaps out of habit, had my favorite professor, favorite poet, favorite alcohol. Afterwards, years after I left Bosnia, I looked for my favorite everywhere. I wanted to be ready, although you and I hadn't talked in a long time and he was gone without a trace.

I had a favorite coffee shop in Dublin, library, store, park, bench, and tree. I had it all; I was complete, but at the same time embarrassed by my childish habit. I had my shape and my color. Now that it didn't matter anymore.

Even the morning I woke up next to Michael after the first time we had sex, while his dog was still whining in the other room. I didn't know what to talk about – the bed that had conveniently united us the night before now revealed that we were complete strangers. I looked at the row of records next to the wall and the first thing that came to my mind was, 'Which one's your favorite?'

He stood up, awkward and hairy as he was, and sauntered down to his beloved vinyls. He pulled out a record I had never seen before – it had a picture of a skull and woman's lips on it.

'This one's my favorite this month,' he said solemnly and set the needle. From the turntable, I heard words which one day I would know by heart, but were completely new to me at that point, their sound bouncing off my naked body in a stranger's bed:

Do you wanna be an angel, do you wanna be a star?
Do you wanna play some magic on my guitar?
Do you wanna be a poet, do you wanna be my string?
You could be anything.

Michael climbed onto the bed and started playing the air guitar above me, strumming his pubic hairs like strings. He sang without a voice, with a virtuoso's grimace on his face. While I laughed, he sneaked under the cover and started biting my thighs. He stayed between my legs long enough to make up for last night's infamous five minutes. And that's how I created our whole relationship – out of a silly question from your seventh birthday.]

six

Sooner or later, eyes get used to darkness. What was thick wool at first, covering everything – Lejla and me, cars, roads, the whole of Bosnia – started fading, thinning. Soon I could tell one silhouette from another. This is a house, this is a tree, this is a stray dog. They regained their limits, the line that made them individual, separate from the rest of the world.

Jajce greeted us with a crooked sign, yellow like a distant planet in the middle of the dark universe, with letters in the Latin and Cyrillic alphabets and tiny genitals someone had added.

Regardless of the darkness, we managed to find Mrs. Knežević's house immediately, thanks to Lejla's infallible photographic memory. Where I saw suspicious paths and unpassable corners, she recognized the way to her *friend from Jajce*. 'Take a left here, straight on . . . the right turn, there next to the kiosk . . .' At that point I realized that both the car and I were nothing but an extension of Lejla's will, she moved us with her words, and we followed obediently.

*

Frozen on her doorstep under a round lamp with a moth dancing in it, Mrs. Knežević looked like the archetype of a different Bosnia – warm and large-breasted – always there to take you into her arms and fill your stomach; to tell you, 'Oh, honey, it's not that bad . . .' She was too old to be seriously considered Lejla's friend, and yet too young to be some forgotten great-aunt I knew nothing about. While I parked in the front yard, which looked like a botanical cemetery – a dead weeping fig here, a dead hydrangea there – Lejla was already hugging her *friend*. They must have met during those twelve years we hadn't been in touch. There was an overdose of affection in their hug, something that couldn't have been older than a year or two, a performance for my eyes only. As if that gesture was meant to tell me that she could get on well with *some* women, how they could understand and love her, the way I never could.

As I approached the house, Mrs. Knežević wiped her hands on the purple apron and shouted, 'Come on, girls, the pie's done . . . Get it while it's warm!'

Lejla replied in cold blood, 'Sara doesn't speak our language. She's from Dublin. I can translate.' And so she sealed my mouth before I had the chance to say anything. Mrs. Knežević looked at me as if I were someone with special needs; she was suddenly full of some love that had been waiting for me – the poor little Irishwoman who got lost in this neck of the woods, who was just about to find out what a real hostess and a real *sirnica* were.

I gave Lejla a sharp look, waiting for her to say she was only kidding, incapable of uttering a single word myself. She had taken my mother tongue away in two seconds, and then coldly took her shoes off and walked into the lit room from which the smell of cheese and fresh dough was escaping. I followed her every step, ready to break her bones the minute I got the chance.

'Ask her if she's ever tried *sirnica*,' Mrs. Knežević yelled from the kitchen. Lejla turned to me and said, in fluent English, though with an ossified accent, that Mrs. Knežević wanted to know whether I was a virgin.

'Lejla, what the fuck? It's not funny . . .' I hissed.

'Shhh! Speak English!' And then she shouted so that her friend would hear her, 'Sara says she simply loves *sirnica*!'

'Oh, right, I forgot you were a spoiled brat,' I said in English, 'do forgive me.' I wanted to embarrass her with my perfect accent, but her cold eyes only revealed the pointlessness of my dumb boasting. We were in Bosnia, where immaculate accents go whoring.

'Well, she's never tasted a better *sirnica*!' our hostess shouted excitedly, which diligent Lejla quickly translated into English for me. 'Mrs. Knežević says she simply loves having Irish whores over.'

She was having fun. The queen of darkness had descended to be among us mortals and live a little. Now we were to dance like monkeys until she got bored and returned to her icy throne. Like that day she hid Dejan's pencil case in the school toilet. I felt sorry for him, the way he screamed and cried for everyone to see. 'My uncle bought it for me in Germany!'

But Lejla just smiled, acting like she had nothing to do with it, drawing Donald Duck by numbers: one, two, three, four – accurately like a surgeon – five, six, and there goes the beak. She had the same evil smile now, except the years had deprived her of the right to be mean. Only the evil remained. But I didn't complain, I accepted that I would be *Sara from Dublin* for that one night in Mrs. Knežević's house. I accepted everything – I would sing, dance, and juggle, as long as we got to Vienna. After that we would be done. She would have to find a new circus troupe for herself.

We were sitting in a small living room where each surface had its own tiny needlepoint cloth cover, as if doilies had fallen like snow all over Mrs. Knežević's place and stayed forever stuck to the TV, the little table, the windowpane. A bunch of smiling faces looked at us from family photos, their eyes and mouths distorted behind the uneven glass of the cabinet. She had ducks everywhere – plastic, ceramic, plush – and their motionless heads were directed towards the TV in the corner. A battered blanket was stretched over the couch where we were sitting. I felt like a tiny piece of finely woven embroidery, a piece of red wool held fast in a tapestry hung on the wall. Everything so warm, so colorful, with a smell hovering between home staleness and old, wrinkled skin.

'Here's the *sirnica*,' Mrs. Knežević said proudly, carrying a large silver tray, which was obviously the best thing she had in the house. She served homemade cherry juice with too little water to dilute it. Two large pieces of the layered pie breathed on the chipped plates that had tiny flowers fading at their edges and two miniature lovers, a shepherd and a shepherdess, holding hands and looking longingly at each other.

When she noticed that I was looking at the embroidered cloth hanging over the TV, covering half of it, Mrs. Knežević bragged to Lejla, 'Tell her I made all of them. It's punch needlework with silk thread, so one strand loop and one active. Not like crochet. So that's the difference.'

I thought she must have had a special room where she kept all the thread and wool, perhaps even some poor sheep in chains. Lejla carried on translating into English, replacing the words *one strand loop* and *crochet* with a convenient *some embroidery shit*. Then she said she had to use the restroom and took her purse from the couch. I shouted cheerfully, 'Why don't you clog your dear friend's toilet with your tampons?' which she ignored completely, leaving me alone with our dedicated hostess.

I smiled at Mrs. Knežević to show my gratitude and took my plate. Well, I thought, at least I won't have to engage in one of those small-talk topics like the weather and cooking. I don't speak *our language*. I can eat in peace.

But before I took my first bite, Mrs. Knežević addressed me, slowly as if she were addressing a child, with all her facial muscles working in order for me to understand.

'Leeelaaa,' she stretched it and pointed a finger at the restroom, 'is a greeeat girrrl.' Then she gave me the thumbs up in order to explain to a stupid Dublin girl what she meant. She was certain that even Irish people could grasp the sublime Slavic semantics as long as you talked to them slowly and patiently. I nodded and went on eating. A great girl, sure. One that threw used tampons out the window. I was almost hoping she would clog the toilet or make some other mess.

With a face frozen in the lady-of-the-house smile, Mrs. Knežević observed my every bite: her eyes moved up and down with my jaw, as if the whole point of our visit was for

me to admit I had never eaten a better pie. I pointed at the
food and raised my thumb, to deliver her from pain.

'Good, right? The word is *dobra*. *Dooo-braa*.'

I repeated *dooo-braaa* obediently, as if hearing the word for
the first time.

'A lovely girl, lovely . . .' Mrs. Knežević went on, this time
addressing the faces in the cabinet, more to herself, like it
didn't really matter whether I could understand or not.

'Dear God, what a lovely voice her father had . . . Like
a nightingale. But it's just terrible the way her brother
ended . . .'

She doesn't know that Armin is in Vienna, I thought. I
stopped chewing. I wanted to say something, but I couldn't,
it would have given me away. I had to be impassive, like one of
those ducks on the shelf, without a language. But something
had jumped inside of me, like a scared hare out of a bush
in the middle of my chest. Armin's in Vienna. That's why
I'm here, why I'm sitting and eating Mrs. Knežević's *sirnica*.
Because *he* is in Vienna. If I repeated that thought too many
times, I thought, it would become pointless, lose its meaning.
Armin would disappear again.

'Everyone knows . . . They don't wanna talk about it.
But everyone knows who took those poor boys that winter,'
Mrs. Knežević went on, now completely sunk into her
thoughts and what she was saying. I felt like I was witness-
ing her personal ritual during which some mantras had to
be spoken again and again, whoever might be listening. Each
word hit my head as if she had thrown photos and ceramic
ducks at me.

'Here I am,' Lejla said and came back to the couch next to me, interrupting Mrs. Knežević's ritual mourning.

'Did you hear that?' I asked quietly, in a foreign tongue. 'She doesn't know that . . .'

'What?'

'That he . . . he's in Vienna.'

'Is she . . . all right in the head?' Mrs. Knežević asked suddenly, pointing her chin at me, all whispers and frowns, not because she was worried I would somehow understand her, but because she had made herself uncomfortable by asking such a question. My dumbness was convincing.

'I'm not all right in the head, I hang out with Lejla Begić, which means I'm a complete idiot,' I said in English, with a smile.

Lejla started laughing between two bites of pie.

'Sara's fine. She's not crazy . . . Completely. If that's what you meant.'

'She must be crazy to come here,' Mrs. Knežević said and took the plate from my hands. 'If I had a place somewhere abroad, I'd never come back here. Dooo youuu want anooother? Another piece? A pieeece?' she asked unexpectedly loudly, pointing at Lejla's pie. I shook my head. I only wanted to find a bed and sleep. Text Michael that I was alive.

'Are we gonna sleep here?' I asked Lejla in English.

'It's too early to sleep.'

'It's pitch dark outside,' I said.

'So what? Do we have to sleep every time it gets dark? How old are you?'

'Older than you,' I replied coldly.

Her English grammar was much better than it used to be. Did she take classes? Travel? And the racket in the car. She started playing tennis and studying English. Who was this woman and in whose car and for whose brother?

'In any case,' she said, 'I wanna see the catacombs.'

'Now? At this hour?'

'Don't be such a granny, it's not even five o'clock.'

The catacombs. A maleficent name for a maleficent little house standing above a hole in the ground. And all that darkness, inside and out. It seemed like everyone thought it was completely normal and I was the only mad one.

We paid a girl at the entrance. She didn't say anything, just put our coins on top of the rest. A little tower of metal. A fee to enter a grave.

Lejla went first, I followed. A child's laughter reached us from deep inside the earth.

'We're not alone,' she said, finally in our language, safe away from her *friend*. There was some excitement in her face, and joy, like she was entering a childhood home, regardless of the dark and the cold that dwelt under all that ground. We descended slowly and safely, her two eyes like the end of an endoscope deep underground.

'Let's go, Mihajlo! Come on!' a woman's voice shouted above us.

And then a child's laughter again, honest but improper, echoing across deep caves, bouncing off walls. You don't laugh in graves, I thought. A loud brat ran out from the underground then, a laughing hyena of a child, sprinting past us and disappearing up onto the surface. We couldn't see him anymore. We were alone in the deep.

'They say there used to be a secret passage,' Lejla said, the same Lejla who more than twenty years ago summoned spirits at a long-gone birthday party. I thought she must be cold in those girly shorts.

She moved from one hole to the next, carefully inspecting the wounds on the walls.

'They say Tito hid here during the Second World War . . . And the passage led to the waterfall,' she said. I wanted to tell her that it was all a bunch of crap to attract tourists. I should have gotten out of there. But it was done – Lejla's magic was still working, after all those years, even underground. She could create an invisible circle that would separate us from the rest of the world. She transformed two separate individuals into *the two of us*, something ours, indivisible, strong and sinewy, spiteful before the whole universe. We were alone underground and I could finally relax. It made no sense to pretend in front of her, to be the well-read translator from Dublin, some cool chick who understood Icelandic movies and prepared vegan canapés for Michael's friends. It made no sense to act. It was just her, the underground, and me. I remembered the island once more. The day I thought she had drowned.

'You got a kid?' she asked suddenly, trying to decipher someone's name engraved in the stone.

'I don't . . . have a kid,' I answered. 'I had the tubes tied.'

She found this interesting enough to stop and look at me. Her eyes were wide in surprise, letting me know she hadn't expected me to do such a thing. To her I was one of those ordinary, boring people who were supposed to succumb to biology compliantly. Her contact lenses travelled from my face all the way to my crotch, as if she would see something there, something missing.

'Wow . . . That some kinda fashion up there in Europe?' she asked.

'It's no fashion at all. I don't want to have children.' I wanted to add, 'It's enough to have you,' but I didn't. She raised her eyebrows and puckered her lips like she was sorry she had even asked in the first place, and moved on to the next hole in the ground. Maybe I could have explained, given her my reasons, but I realized it would have been futile. Some people want to be continued, to keep swimming inside someone else's cells long after they're dead. And I only wanted to stop. I wanted *myself* to be the only kind of *I* that ever existed. She wouldn't have understood. She, who spread out infinitely.

'Is it enough now? Can we go?' I asked.

She walked past me and caressed my cheek, just like that. Like she had recognized me in that darkness, for the first time since I had gotten back. She decided I needed a touch.

'Let's go,' she said.

Later that night, as I was lying in the big marital bed of Mrs. Knežević (who, like a true hostess, slept crumpled up on the couch), I wanted to get my courage up and finally ask Lejla why Armin was in Vienna, why he hadn't called. I watched her comb her long white hair with sharp moves, as if wanting to liberate it from the sticky darkness and tiny insects. Then she took those tiny rags off, got her legs under the thin cover, and turned her back to me with a yawned *good night*. I only managed to say, 'Lejla.' I said it so quietly that she didn't hear me. When I thought I was ready to say his name in front of her, she was already sleeping. I could see her ribs – they stretched her delicate, suntanned skin. A green bruise went up and down, like a bit of sea within reach of my hand. She slept the same way she used to sleep – like she was dead. That summer, on the island, as the olive tree slapped our window, I lay next to Lejla's inert body and knew that something had finished. Alcohol had made her sleepy just like it had made me cry.

It has always been that way.

A new Lejla was sleeping next to me now. Older and colder, but still with that previous one crouching somewhere between her ribs. I couldn't tell her hair from the whiteness of the pillow. Two equally strong wishes battled inside me: one logical, grownup – to sneak out, make my way to the road, and hitchhike to Zagreb; the other mad, inconsistent, from the bottom of my cold womb – to get close to her, hold her, and to sleep in her white hair like a penitent puppy. In the end I only stared at the ceiling until the sound of crickets from the dead front yard lulled me to sleep. A giant plush duck looked at me from the armchair in the corner. Maybe that's *Mister* Knežević, I thought, right before I fell asleep.

[I think we were eight. Or nine. Doesn't really matter, anyway. I only know we were the same age because that was possible only in the pocket of time between late winter and early spring. May would come afterwards and I would get ahead of you with the over-the-top birthday parties my mother organized. There were tasteless fruitcakes, tailor-made dresses, and board games nobody cared for. As if she had prepared celebrations for a little dictator. But before all that, only briefly, between your January and my May, we would be the same age and I would always feel a sense of peace, as if I had finally swum to that tiny island where we were a bit more alike than usual. It was the same that winter when we were eight, or maybe nine.

The world, at least the small corner of it we referred to as such, smelled differently. Of different food, different fabric softener. Different than when the smells disappeared. But this memory is not about the darkness that came after. This memory is about the winter when I killed the sparrow.

I never told anyone about it. Not even the cheapest therapist I could find in Dublin. It seemed like she was much more interested in my mother than me. We talked about my parents, about Michael, even you and Armin. But never about the sparrow I killed that winter when we were eight, or maybe nine. How does that story begin? You're not here, it's all up to me.

I have to turn to my frozen lake again and stomp on the surface with my heel until a crack appears. There it is – a small one. You can't say I'm making this up.

The first memory: a little eye looking at me from the snow. Everything is born from that look. Your black eyes standing to the side, not blinking.

I remember the smell of snow, the touch of rough woolly mittens and what your mom called *a toothy sun*. I remember us squinting at all that whiteness and how it was marked here and there by traces of mud and children's footsteps.

We liked to dress 'seriously' back then. It was your idea. You started wearing dress pants; you would tuck your shirt in and braid your hair so tightly that it stretched your face and narrowed your eyes. I mocked you at first. 'You dress like my dad,' I told you.

'If you wanna dress like a small child, that's your problem.'

That's all you said. I never forgot that. And then you went on copying numbers from the blackboard to the square-lined notebook.

The 'small child' comment came back to me one morning in Dublin before my first job interview. I braided my hair and tucked my shirt in. All those remnants of you, mutilated by time and my lazy memory, made their way into distant routines when I least expected it. Sometimes I would open the door and let them in. Sometimes I would persuade myself that I wasn't remembering it right, it wasn't like that, and so I would discredit everything you were to me. I wanted to find something originally *mine*, something born and raised outside of your influence, and clean it of you, wash it like an avocado seed.

Don't go off topic, your black eyes tell me. This is important.

You're right. This is the day I killed the sparrow. I decided to dress seriously because of you, so that I wasn't 'a small child'. It was not that hard – mom was happy to use all the 'skirt suits' as she called them, the ones my aunts had given me for birthdays. We must have looked ridiculous to other children, but it didn't bother us. We were certain everyone around us was stupid. *We* were serious. Our shoes had laces, not straps. How long did that phase last? Probably until the summer that year when we couldn't wait to get back into shorts and start scratching our knees on the hill behind the school.

I can't remember what the teacher looked like. I can't remember our classroom, either, or half of the students in it. But I do know you had a metallic pencil case with a pale Coca-Cola bottle illustrated on top. Your little sharpener clanked around it when you moved it. And your two pencils, one for sketching, the other for writing. Nobody else had a pencil for sketching.

'Armin says you can't draw with a regular pencil,' you explained.

And who knows how many other things. Armin says this, Armin says that. I asked my mom to buy me a sketching pencil. She brought home from work the same pencil I already had.

I remember it was cold that day I killed the sparrow. Colder than usual. Or perhaps not, perhaps that's a subsequent figment. I was wearing woolly gloves that pricked me and an orange scarf over my wet nose. Dad had given me that scarf and told me it was the best brand – I had to take good care of it. I would come to school, take it off gently, like a live fox, and slowly fold it on the table before putting it in my backpack. During lunch break I would take it out and wrap it around my neck again. There was a safety in that scarf that hid half of my face. It was easy to talk to other kids behind its wool. After all, it was the best brand, as Dad had explained.

I was wearing it the day I killed the sparrow. I know you remember it too, though we never discussed it. We went out during lunch break. We split your bread roll and my chocolate. We would each bite the apple once and throw it over the fence. Dejan was there. Rade, too. And a few more boys from our class. They looked at us girls with contempt in their eyes, ready to accept a power given to them unfairly. They had no idea what to do with it. And we felt the injustice as if someone else had been given a complicated toy we would have been able to put together in two seconds.

They were the main characters in adventures that, to our jealous ears, sounded much more spectacular than they could have been. They told us they went hunting with Grandpa over the weekend, and we pictured bloodthirsty beasts falling under their precise bullets. They said they made wooden birdhouses in the treetops, and we saw mighty eagles sleeping in freshly polished apartments. They bragged about how their fathers let them shoot cans behind the house, and how they were allowed to try beer from those cans, their dads patting their backs proudly. Back then that *beer* sounded like an unattainable nectar of the gods, something that made boys more important than us.

That day they were bullying Jovana because of the hair on her legs.

I was laughing, you rolled your eyes. I didn't find it funny, I just wanted those boys to like me. I wanted to be a part of some group, for everyone to think I was *with them* at lunch break, although this time it was completely accidental. I was digging a shortcut to the world of men, hungry for their presence and acceptance. That desire – to belong to someone – put everything else in shadow.

You told me you invited Dejan to your birthday parties only because your mom made you do it. And I wondered why anyone wouldn't want Dejan at their birthday. I was always happy to see my peers around, to see another kid in my room. When did I realize that children could be bad people? Later, probably, when the darkness arrived. When they moved on from Jovana's legs to you. Dejan, Rade, Miroslav, and Aljoša. They started mocking you the minute you changed your name. They would tear a sheet of paper out from a notebook, blow their snot into it, and then crumple it up and throw it at you. On your Reader textbook they carved a poor reproduction of the Serbian coat of arms with four Cyrillic letter Ss in its corners. ('Stupid swine scribble shit.' Armin explained the meaning of the mysterious sign. 'I thought that was the letter C, not S,' you said, annoyed that a single letter can mean so many things.) But you weren't Jovana – you hit back just as hard. You threw their backpacks through the window, you undid their shoelaces, you hid their pencil cases and notebooks in dirty school toilets. When the time came for me to choose – you or them – something won me over to your side. Maybe Armin, maybe something else. Perhaps the fact that you were the only one who had interpreted my crime correctly. As long as I was your friend, you wouldn't use it against me. Maybe that's why I chose you, or maybe for something less noticeable. Something that surfaced along with your black hair, years later, on that damn island.

And the sparrow was so small, smaller than my eight-year-old fist. In fact, it didn't even resemble a sparrow. It looked like someone had randomly stuck little puffs of gray wool over its ruddy skin. Its eyes were blurred somehow, getting used to the world. There was something terrifying about the little monster and its pleading beak. With its blind eyes it looked for a bit of food, a bit of life. It must have fallen from a nest; it had a broken wing and a weirdly crooked leg.

Snow had gathered by the school fence. The principal scolded us for eating it. 'A disgusting habit. I simply can't understand it,' she said scornfully during the parents' meeting, as if our mothers had cooked the snow for us. But we didn't pay attention to her or our parents. The snow was clean and cold. It screeched when it touched the teeth and then melted over the warm tongue, leaving behind the metallic taste of the sky. You ate the most. Whole fistfuls of snow disappeared in your mouth. One time I made you laugh so hard that you spat it straight on my face. And then we laughed even harder. It was the first year of our friendship, only we didn't think that way then. Nobody thinks that way when some stories start.

You can't know it's the first chapter. In that moment, it is the whole time and the whole story, there's nothing before or after. A red cap taming your black hair. Your gloves with ten fingers because 'small children' wore mittens with only a thumb. Blue rubber boots you couldn't stand, but your mom made you wear them to keep your pants from getting soaked. Your birthday and the summoning of spirits. Making paper dolls. That was it. And then I killed the sparrow.

I don't know who started it. They dragged it in the snow, played catch with its helpless body. Rade threw it in the air and squealed, 'I'm flying, I'm flying,' then, 'Oops, I fell,' which made Dejan laugh madly. They were holding the bird by its tiny leg as if they were afraid that the horror of its fragile life would pass onto them. They threw it at each other and dodged its touch. Then they got tired and laid it on a small heap of snow.

You were standing to the side, quiet. You wanted to leave, but I longed to stay, to be part of the *gang*. It got on my nerves how frozen you were – not a smile, not a single joke. I didn't want them to make a connection between me and your coldness. I laughed without wanting to, dodging your eyes.

We thought the bird was dead, but then it opened one blind eye. 'Who's gonna put him out of his misery?' Dejan asked and everyone went quiet. 'What is it, Rade? You a pussy?'

But the other boy just stared at the snow palely, it wasn't fun anymore. I didn't want to look at you, but could feel you watching me. As if you had known, in advance, before everyone, before me, what I was about to do. As if it had already happened in your head, there was no stopping it.

I crushed it. My boot dived into the snow while my hot foot pulsated wildly. Mom made me wear double socks. But I could feel something breaking underneath. I could feel the soft feathers and fragile bones and the little blurry eye sticking to my sole. I had to clean the boot with snow later. A trace of blood remained and a few feathers. Dejan tapped my back and said, 'At least Sara isn't a pussy.' The others just kept standing and staring at the hole in the snow, at my boot, at me. And I was afraid, though I didn't know of what exactly. There was no rule stating we weren't supposed to kill wounded birds. This one was already half-dead, fallen from the nest, it didn't stand a chance in that snow. Hadn't the boys already finished it off with their dumb game? Hadn't it already died before I stepped on it? Hadn't I *put it out of its misery?* And yet I was afraid of some invisible law. Dejan's approval, which I so longed for, was suddenly nothing but the blabbering of a brat who witnessed my crime. It must be set down somewhere, I thought, someone somewhere knows. A little beak opening and closing; little undeveloped wings. Somewhere it *must* be written that it was wrong.

I looked up and saw your face. I can't remember what you looked like as a child. You're always the same to me. Whenever I think of the moment I killed the sparrow and looked at you, I see an older you, your hair changes color, eyes too. Black braids turn blonde, like that day in college, then white, like in the Astra. Black eyes sparkle with a bluish tinge, like the contact lenses that would come later. I can't see your eyes in that memory, nor your nose, lips, hair, but I remember the look on your face. You were staring at the hole in the snow, where the crushed sparrow lay, as if it had sucked in all the meaning from everything that surrounded us. If we got too close to the tiny uncovered grave, it would suck us in too. Everything became pointless: our serious shirts, our rubber boots, our sketching pencils, the school and the teacher and the classmates. In your eyes, I'd deprived everything of its purpose. That's when I realized what I had done, not before I saw that look on your face. I realized I had done something wrong, something I wasn't supposed to do, and which had nothing to do with the sparrow or the fact it had already been almost dead.

We went home afterwards, and back to school the next day. Things went on as usual. We shared the table, we shared our crayons, and we laughed at the boys. You helped me with math, I helped you with reading and writing. You never once mentioned my crime. And yet I knew something was different. Only one side of your mouth laughed now. A bit of darkness sneaked into your pupils. I had taken something from you that winter, something you can only take once, because it exists only once.

You came to my birthday party in early May. 'This is my best friend – Lejla,' I said proudly to my mom, as if I had made you out of thin air. And Mom said nothing, but dragged me to Maša Čeković's house that weekend for a playdate. All of my parents' friends had boys, so Mom had to leaf through her small fake-leather address book until she stumbled upon C and cheerfully shouted, 'Well, of course, Doctor Čeković! They have a daughter, right?'

I was ready to do my part. It had crossed my mind that perhaps Maša and I were made for each other, that you had been nothing but an unlucky coincidence. I would get a new friend. She doesn't know I killed the sparrow. I'm allowed a second beginning.

However, Maša spent the whole afternoon in a corner with a coloring book in her hands, saying nothing. I played with her Barbies on the other side of the spacious room. She had a whole bunch of those dolls: blonde, dark-haired, and ginger. Every now and then she would look up from her coloring book to check what I was up to. Whether I was pulling a tight dress over Barbie's hips or putting a tiny comb through Ken's hair, she would look at me like I was crazy, like nothing I did made sense to her. What did she do to those dolls, I thought, if dressing and combing were so weird? I kept eyeing the door, hoping my mom would appear and tell me we were going home. But the only thing that came into the room was the laughter of adults tolerating each other for the sake of their kids. After a long time spent in unbearable silence, she finally spoke in a deep, accomplice's voice.

'I have a secret. Wanna see it?'

I thought that perhaps everything was not lost – we would become close now, I could forget about you and the dead sparrow.

Once I nodded, Maša took a tiny matchbox from underneath her bed. I moved closer to her on the parquet floor and she raised the box to the height of our eyes and half opened it.

I screamed. There was a tiny live cockroach inside it. When she saw the expression I made, Maša shut the box fast and said coldly, 'If you tell my mom, I will kill you. One word.'

That night my mom tucked me in and gently asked whether I liked my new friend. I could see only a row of her white teeth sparkling in the room's darkness. I wanted the sight to linger – a grin without a mother was better than a mother without a grin. I replied that I had a nice time playing with Maša. The streetlight bounced off her crooked front tooth. She whispered *good night* and kissed my forehead, the way those mothers in American movies did. The minute she left the room and closed the door, I whispered quickly into the dark, 'Lejla is my best friend!' Like it was important to say it, like someone would listen, someone who knew I had killed the sparrow, someone I couldn't fool. One of those terrible ghosts that move through the ceiling when they hear your spells. With my ridiculous mantra, I wanted to grow an invisible barrier around myself in order to be safe and able to fall asleep. That sentence protected me from my mother's white teeth. It protected me, too, from the little cockroach fidgeting that night in the matchbox under Maša Čeković's bed.]

seven

That night, in the warm broad bed of Mrs. Knežević, I dreamed of a sunny day and a field, a botanical miracle, as if from a Japanese commercial. Lejla and I were sitting at a big wooden desk, in the middle of the field, cutting dresses out of fashion magazines. I was trying to cut down the edges, but kept dropping the scissors, mutilating tiny two-dimensional women. The landscape stretched infinitely; there wasn't a hill or a house in sight, only the field and our desk. In the dream, I had peacefully accepted that this was all, that nothing else existed. I didn't need more.

All of Mrs. Knežević's ducks had gathered around us – ceramic, plush, plastic: completely motionless, but with lively eyes moving left and right. They followed everything we were doing. I was angry with Lejla in the dream, but I don't know why. I wanted to shout in our language, to give myself away in front of those ducks, but couldn't utter a single word. Her hair was black. And her eyes. Like that day on the island. She opened a big tote bag and pulled a tiny raven out. He was small, quivering as if my face scared him. He made himself small in Lejla's hands, horrified by my presence. She looked at

me worryingly and opened her mouth as if to ask me something. Then I woke up.

I was alone in the bed. It suddenly crossed my mind that
she had run away from me, headed for Vienna on foot. I had
forgiven her all the silliness in the two seconds it took me to
flee the room and realize she was in the bathroom. My own
fear surprised me. A part of me wanted to get rid of her, throw
her out of the car window onto the dirt road like an empty
can. But the other part of me feared her absence. She was no
longer just Lejla. Now she was Armin, too, and Vienna, and
the end of the story. I wasn't ready to give all that up. I only
wanted to get back in the Astra and keep moving.

Having said goodbye to Mrs. Knežević, who had wiped her
hands on her purple apron in order to give me a big hug, we
went to the AVNOJ Museum, as I had promised. It was cold
there, in that silly, mute meeting with its empty chairs. Lejla
trailed her fingertips over the wooden benches and chairs.
Chipped blue nail polish. A white bun on top of her head like
a sleeping polar animal. I was looking at her; she was looking
at flags. Russia. The USA.

A mole I had forgotten, on the back of her neck. Great
Britain. France. That day on the island. She, floating on the
surface of the water. Yugoslavia.

And some people around us, silent nostalgiacs with frozen
smiles and cell phones in the air. Taking pictures of history.
Taking pictures of pictures. Comrade Marx, Comrade Stalin.
I took my own phone from my pocket. One photo for Michael.
But the battery was empty and the phone went black the
second I unlocked it. I would have to remember the place the
best I could, I thought. No help from technology. Not because

of the stone giant frowning in the corner, nor the Antifascist Declaration of the People of Yugoslavia. I would have to remember it for her sake – for Lejla. What if she, too, split apart into pieces of old rags with tiny stars and pale colors?

She observed all that emptiness with a kind of disappointment. As if she had expected something. Something was supposed to be there. She had been excited before we got in. Her broken 'Internationale', although she still hadn't learned how to whistle. The morning was dark, a bit less than the previous day, but still deprived of sunlight. Yet, inside that building, circular white lamps hung, giving off neon light from a different time. The flags lay flaccid, free from rogue winds – nothing could wave them anymore.

She took the blue chewing gum, the size of a chestnut, out of her mouth and stuck it on the back of Tito's armchair. She gave me a look over her shoulder, in order to make sure I had witnessed the transgression. Proud of her minute crime, she smiled crookedly, but something sneaked out from her face and gave her away. One Lejla – who couldn't care less, who proved her supremacy by sticking gum on historical artifacts – was overshadowed by a different one who wouldn't admit she was disappointed. She had expected something; she came there for a reason. The answer was right under my nose and it eluded me, though I was there with her. Even those tourists had disappeared. Only the two of us and the big stone Marshal who couldn't look us in the eye. Both of them exhausted, Lejla and Josip. *If you look closely, you can see his eye between two pieces of paprika.* But there was nothing there, just some dead words laughing at us from the walls. *Long live our allies.*

She was never one for nostalgia. Lejla was someone who found the past about as relevant as discarded tampons left behind somewhere in the grass.

She would brush memories off her jeans like breadcrumbs. If it wasn't in front of her, if it wasn't what was coming up, why waste the energy? But there was something there, some story she had believed, and she couldn't hide it. Her eyes were defeated. In that pointless room, she resembled a child who had organized a tea party that nobody came to. The seats were empty. Plaster was peeling off the walls. A plastic Disneyland, unworthy of the fairytales that preceded it. A *happy-meal* Yugoslavia.

'I need to use the toilet,' she said quickly and left the room. The whole meaning of that place followed her out. Officers' chairs became nothing more than a pile of old wood. Flags suddenly became rags. As if she had taken Yugoslavia with her.

I waited outside in that twilight I couldn't yet grasp, but slowly learned to accept. It was *our* darkness, something familiar, which fogged our borders and hid the roads. After someone else's light bulbs from another era, someone's dried-up Atlantis, the darkness soothed my eyes. It was mine. Wrong and repulsive, but still mine. Something real, out of the wrapper. Something ours.

'Let's go,' she said. And that was it. No comrades, no allies – alone. Back in the Astra, back on the road. Only this time with a different Lejla. She had left the playful waitress there in the AVNOJ meeting place, to walk between the chairs, serve tea, and flirt with important ghosts. She pressed her forehead against the window and stared at the dark, at the deformed silhouettes of trees, at the disfigured signs by side of the road, and the crystal pixels on the river. Rocks peeked through the night like cold neglected breasts. I didn't dare break the silence. The woman next to me was a reflection of something I knew, that serious schoolgirl sitting by me, figuring out the math on the blackboard. I'm not talking about appearance, clothes, or behavior. That *something* about her is like a color. I'm not sure which one; I can't define her according to a numerical convention on a spectrum. She evades that. Facing her, all words are miserably colorblind.

I drove slowly, afraid of animals coming out of the dark, monsters jumping out of the river, other cars rushing down the road because they were better prepared for the impenetrable dusk. I didn't need her to talk to me, to explain what exactly had taken place in the museum; it was enough to be part of something with her, by her. To think – Lejla and I are driving, Lejla and I are in a car, Lejla and I are going to Vienna. That subject, *Lejla and I*, ripped apart on the island, after that terrible day. I had broken it. But now there was a new *Lejla and I*. Different, clumsily joined like two pieces of broken crockery, with a crack down the middle that could never be concealed. Chipped, imperfect, but still whole.

She was silent almost all the way to Krupa; I thought she had fallen asleep leaning on the window. But after a while she gave a sudden start, as if she had remembered something, and opened the glove box in front of her. A few tapes fell out. She inspected them seriously as if buying jewelry then rolled down the window and started throwing out everything that failed to interest her.

'Do you have to throw everything out the window? Do you have any idea how long it takes for all that plastic to decompose in nature?' I asked.

'How long? Go on, enlighten me,' she replied solemnly, still rummaging through the tapes.

'Well, I don't know . . . Hundreds of years. A thousand maybe.'

'At least we'll leave something behind,' she said and, after four or five rejected tapes, picked one and pushed it in the player. A squeal came out first, so morose that I thought the player wasn't working. And then, from some tenth or eleventh birthday party, from that ghostly country with white lamps, a young woman's voice sighed:

My baby is dangerous, but he's so sweet.
He's so very naughty, he's got devil's feet.
One hand, two hands, right under my dress.
Well, baby, that ain't right. You're making a mess!

'Lejla, you're fucking with me.'

Tajči. She played damn Tajči. And then she started singing with a duckface, '*He wears a cowboy jacket, and drinks beer with no foam . . .*'

'I can't believe this,' I said.

She started nudging me. 'Come on, Sara . . .'

'No fucking way,' I said. All of Michael's records flashed before my eyes: Dylan. Cohen. Pink Floyd. I'm from Dublin, I have an avocado tree, and I'm cool. I know *Blonde on Blonde* by heart. I don't sing Tajči. But she went on, '*He's got sadness in his eyes . . . but loves me alone . . .*'

And so on. After that, we heard 'Fall in Love With My Eyes', and Lejla, for some reason, took particular delight in singing the song with the soft Croatian *ch*. There was only Tajči on the tape. I didn't want to admit I knew all the words.

'How old is she now?' I asked to stop her singing.

'Who? Tajči? No idea . . .'

'I guess she must be near fifty. I think she lives abroad somewhere,' I said.

'Who cares?' she asked, and went on singing.

And so we continued the journey through the all-consuming darkness: the Astra crawled along the river like a stray cur, with early Tatjana Matejaš Tajči hits rendered in Lejla's atonal interpretation. After a while the sweet tune started carrying me like a simple ritual chant. The road curved ahead like an exotic dancer. The dusk became deeper, although it was barely after noon. I had to slow down and concentrate in order to drive. I had forgotten where we were heading. We had left the second session of the AVNOJ and were now fleeing towards the Axis powers with sugary chords from the early nineties. It didn't matter where we were going. Just like the tennis racket behind us, or her wedding band hanging from the air freshener. There was no longer a Michael, or a Dino. We were moving, pushing on, being safe in the progressive. Perhaps that's why she had called me. No one else would have known how to shut up and drive, how to listen to Tajči. Though perhaps I imagined that. It's quite possible I was nothing more than a driving license and a full wallet. I didn't care. I could be anything and the journey would go on toward what we couldn't name, yet were both thinking of. We said Mostar, we said Zagreb, we said Vienna. But not that. Lejla was singing, I was driving, as if nothing was waiting ahead. And she was there. Like darkness at the end of the tunnel, irrevocable and inevitable. A cold grave in the middle of our itinerary. A cleverly concealed ulcer. Banja Luka.

I wanted to drive past as if I hadn't known her, as if nothing of importance had ever happened there. That way I would have turned her into one of those towns whose names on the map mean nothing to you. A cartographer might just as well erase them, you wouldn't even notice. But Lejla was faster. She said, 'Can we stop at home?'

At home. Two words and a whole town grew out of the map. It got its streets and buildings, its school, Gymnasium, Faculty of Philosophy. A river cut through its skin and belted itself with bridges. Vines sprouted from graves. Windows broke through walls on their own and lit lamps behind their blurry glass. Somewhere a TV was on. And all that because Lejla said *at home.* There, where people disappeared, rabbits died, and no avocado ever grew. She pulled Banja Luka out of the earth in two words. There was no more music in the car. Tajči had run out of hits, wiped her makeup off, packed her bags and moved to America.

I made a turn from the through road to the Gymnasium. A traffic light stopped us. Lejla stared at the red bricks, frowned, and said, 'Remember prom?'

'I do,' I said. Of course I do. *Gaudeamus igitur.* Waking up alone and deflowered. A tiny white glove floating in the water. We're going to the market to buy a white rabbit.

'What a disgusting night, geez . . . Remember? There, by the river?' she asked, still frowning.

'What are you talking about, it wasn't that bad at all. As far as I remember, you liked it.'

At this, she looked at me as if I had completely lost my mind.

'Liked it?!' She shivered, as if to shake off a dirty curse, and added a firm, 'Yuck.'

'I didn't know you had such a bad time.'

'Well, I guess you don't know everything,' she said and started going through her bag, looking for a new piece of gum.

'Remember those ridiculous ties they were wearing?' I asked.

'That was your guy. And he even gave you flowers.'

'He didn't give me flowers . . . Wait . . . Did he give me flowers?'

'He did. God, your memory's terrible, Sara. He gave you roses. And he wore a tie for you. He was nuts about you. Mine was a total disaster. And every time I see this stupid building I remember his tiny red cock.'

The Gymnasium reminded me of something entirely different. I remembered my first boyfriend, Aleksandar, who put his tongue in my mouth, there in front of that gate. I was sitting in the hole in the wall. He had a beard and a mustache, smelled of cigarettes and cologne. He put his hand under my skirt. It was warm. I was fifteen and thought I knew everything. I wore flannel shirts and ripped denim skirts. I pretended I understood the music of EKV, a new-wave band from Belgrade. I was certain I could draw. I rolled my eyes. There, in front of that decrepit redbrick building, which now gaped empty in a different kind of dark.

The traffic light was red for too long. An old man was trudging down the sidewalk, pulling a one-wheeled trolley behind. There was something white inside it, something I couldn't see. He walked slowly, as if he had to peel his feet off the ground. He was the only human thing in the dark, yet so unlike a human being. It looked like he and the trolley behind him had morphed into one, like a silent wind had moved him, a cruel deity's invisible will. When the traffic lights changed, I sped up to reach him and see what he was dragging behind. It was pitch black, but I managed to see – he was dragging a pig. Dead or maimed, I couldn't tell. A huge, well-fed pig in a wobbly trolley. The man raised his head, but I hit the gas and drove off before he could see me. I didn't want him to look at me.

Lejla's street looked the same as that last night when we buried Hare. I parked two houses down. I didn't want to see the entrance to her yard with the radioactive cherry tree. I didn't want to see their front door with the brass letter R. And least of all did I want to see the biology teacher's balcony or, even worse, himself.

'Come with me,' she said. I thought of her mother, probably thinner than ever, in that pale blackness, with arms like plucked-out wings.

'No, that's OK, you go. I'll meet you later.'

She didn't try to persuade me. She untied her hair and quickly, her hands like two crafty spiders, made a perfect braid. Then she left the car and ironed her T-shirt with her palms. She pulled the tiny shorts down to cover her ass.

'Meet you at Ranko's?'

'Ranko's is fine,' I said and smiled. 'When?'

'In two, three hours?'

'OK.'

She waved and started walking to her yard. I looked at her back as she moved down the street. Thick dusk melted her white hair like a bit of chalk in the hand.

[You recognized numbers on the high-school blackboard as if they were family photographs. Those trails of digits were impenetrable to me; I wanted letters to scoop them into words and make sentences. Our Serbian teacher asked me to write an essay for the school magazine. The subject was 'What I Dream Of'. None of what I wrote was true, but the teacher loved *the writing*. Dad tore the page out later, framed it, and hung it on the dining-room wall. But to you words had long lost their meaning, like empty jars in the pantry. They followed unfair, human laws; their nature changed with each new dictionary. Next to your eternal, unchangeable digits, words were nothing but toothless whores standing before Greek goddesses. So the deal was obvious: you would do two math tests, one under your name and the other under mine, whereas I would write two Serbian compositions. 'Autumn in My Town'. We would change our handwriting to do this properly – you would add serifs and big round bellies to *my* numbers, and I would tilt *your* letters, lengthen their limbs, draw fine lines which my own letters didn't have. I imagined I was you as I wrote essays for Lela Berić. It was during those rare, precious moments that your story really belonged to me and my pencil alone.

'All right. Let's see what we've got now,' our math teacher says. 'Anything interesting here?'

He sat on the table, looking at the blackboard. He's one of those young teachers who try hard to be our *friends*. He's sitting on the desk thinking we like that. Wears a red sports cap. Winks at us.

'What's interesting about *that*,' I whisper.

'Later you're gonna bother me because you're not listening.'

'Seriously, Lejla. What's interesting? I don't get it.'

'The common factor is a+1. See how it's repeated three times? It means you can put it outside the brackets.'

'But then there's only one, and there were three. That doesn't make sense,' I say, confused, and you roll your eyes. I said something stupid, I can tell by your face. And yet I still can't grasp a law that can turn three letters into one. And nobody gives a damn.

The teacher turns around and sighs. 'You two again . . . Come on, which one's coming to the blackboard?'

While I am muttering in defense, you have already got up. You go to the board, glance at the last line of numbers, and add the result in your tiny handwriting.

'That's . . . correct. And now can we see how you got there? So we actually *learn* something today.'

'Isn't it obvious?' you ask seriously, twisting your foot. Two girls in front of my desk exchange mean glances.

'OK, but . . . We haven't seen the process.'

'Do we have to see everything?'

'Indulge me,' the teacher asks, and you roll your eyes, trying not to laugh. You wipe the result and add the four lines you had skipped before, launching thirty mad pencils behind you.

He praises the work and you come back and sit next to me. Quietly, I start copying the equations from the blackboard into my expensive hardback notebook. I can't understand anything. My nipples hurt. Aleksandar had been twisting them the night before. You might know math, but I have a boyfriend. An *older* boyfriend. I let him put his hand between my legs, over leggings. He pushed me against the wall behind the school, panting and sighing, and I copied him, all the while trying to figure out which parts to tell you and which to keep to myself. I told him to be quiet, if a police officer walked by my dad would find out the same day. But Aleksandar said he didn't care, though he stopped kissing me every now and then to check if anyone was coming.

I calculated that we had a few years left before I turned eighteen and we could elope. We would go to Italy because they had cheap spaghetti, the sea, and some buildings Aleksandar had learned about in college. I imagined your envy and enjoyed my future power. I wanted to be the one who would leave. You would have to ask to come visit. I imagined your wide eyes staring at my Italian apartment, my expensive shoes and purses, the latest music tapes. My plan was to take you out for dinner where I would be speaking fluent Italian and you would beg me to translate. 'My friend doesn't speak our language,' I would tell the hot waiter, and you would just stare at us dumbly. No math would help you.

The following week you come to school buttoned up to the neck. Your hair is meticulously gathered in a smooth black bun. You sit down and open your bag so clumsily that all the textbooks fall out.

'What's wrong with you?' I whisper, as you put the things back in your backpack.

'Nothing. There's nothing wrong.'

'You look like a prison guard. On cocaine.'

You cast a quick glance at the teacher, then at me.

'Sara, can I ask you something? You and Aco . . .'

'Yeah?'

'Do you ever feel with him . . . I mean, how should I put it . . . Do you feel something between your legs, you know?'

'He put his hand there, if that's what you mean. That's normal, all couples do that.'

'Yeah, but . . . I'm not talking about that.'

You look at the teacher again. I don't know how to react to your flustered face. I have never been in the position of having to explain something to *you*.

'I had this weird dream last night,' you whisper, 'and I woke up . . . like all . . .'

'You had a nightmare?'

'No. It was nice. Like hot . . . down here, between my legs, you know? And wet.'

'You pissed yourself?'

'Sara, stop fucking around. Listen to me.'

The teacher stands up and starts writing new equations on the blackboard. I think this would make you stop, you always found numbers more interesting than me. But this time you hardly notice them and keep speaking in a low voice.

'It was like . . . hot down there, you know? Like ticklish . . . and like it wanted to get out. And you want it to happen . . . but at the same time it's like it's gonna break you in half . . . if you let it out.'

'Lejla, I've no idea what you're talking about. You're losing it.'

'OK, listen. You know how men . . . When that thing comes out . . . I mean down there, after sex.'

'Sperm?' I say proudly. I read about it in *Teen* magazine the previous summer.

'Yes, that.'

'But you're not a man.'

'Yeah, but . . . I felt it. You know? I think that's it.'

'Lejla, sorry, but you have no idea what you're talking about. Women don't have that. I've had a boyfriend for almost a year so I know what I'm saying.'

'You don't believe me.'

'There's nothing to believe. You woke up sweating, that's all. It happens.'

The teacher looks at us so we shut up and start copying the algebra from the blackboard. We wait for him to look away again. Once you have solved all the equations, you let me copy them from your notebook and speak, in a barely audible mutter, 'I'll tell you what I dreamed about. But it's a secret, OK?'

'Geez, Lejla, who would I tell?'

You pull your chair closer to mine.

'I dreamed I was taking a shower with the math teacher. We were naked. He washed my hair . . . and my back . . . and he washed me down there, you know.'

I can feel my eyeballs dry up, as the teacher's chalk squeals across the blackboard. And you just go on, 'And then he kneeled down . . . And slowly spread my legs.' You stop and swallow. I keep staring as if you were a horror movie.

'What happened next?'

'He kissed me.'

'Down there?! Gross!'

Dead serious, as if you were confirming you had seen aliens land on our planet, you answer, 'Down. There.'

We walk home afterwards. You join me down the Alley because I have persuaded you to help me with math homework. And you still want to talk about your dream and your crotch although I'm stubbornly trying to change the topic. I feel cheated, as if you managed to win the race again. You will find a way to beat my real experience with a dreamed one.

It wasn't fair. I turned fifteen and let Aco touch me over leggings. Boys just stared at you as if you were a complicated dessert surrounded by unknown tableware. You outgrew me that summer, at fourteen, pulled ahead by an unfair law, suddenly a bit closer to the sky than I was. Your hair smelled different. You had breasts. I couldn't let you win again.

'Lejla, that's just nonsense,' I interrupted you. 'You've never kissed anyone.'

'What does that have to do with . . .'

'There's an order to these things,' I explained. 'First the kiss. Then he can grab your butt. Then your boobs. First over the T-shirt, then under. Then you can touch his thing. Then over the leggings. After a year you let him put his hand down your pants. And you haven't even kissed yet.'

We were passing by the monument to the fallen Yugoslav heroes of the Second World War. A mute circle of stone Partisans observed us. You took your backpack off and laid it on the ground, then approached the nearest hero and kissed him on the lips. I rolled my eyes.

'Not like that.'

'Well, show me then,' you said.

'What, now? Here?'

'Yes, here. Kiss . . .' you stopped to read the name. 'Kiss Ranko Šipka.'

I was embarrassed to kiss a dead bust, but I had no choice. I enjoyed the assumption that I had to teach *you* something. Approaching the hero, I touched his cap and slid my fingers slowly down his firm cheeks.

I had to stand on my toes to reach him. Looking into his blind eyes, I touched his stone lips with my tongue. Then I hugged him and pressed myself hard against his cold uniform, joining our lips. And you stared at us, speechless and dedicated, as if trying to solve another algebra equation.

The peace treaty was signed in winter that year. Aleksandar's 'steady girlfriend' was pregnant. Up until that moment I had felt like an extra without a director to guide me. I wasn't sure what I was supposed to be. Now, suddenly, I had an easy supporting role – poor Sara. At least I knew how to play it, thanks to Mom. But you wouldn't let me bed down into my drama. You told me it was stupid to cry in a moment like that.

'Moment like what?' I asked.

'Well, it's over. There's peace. Don't you watch television?'

'What the hell do I care about that?'

You stared into the distance, at the naked branches of slim plane trees, at a building whose graffiti read *out with the mujahedeen!* Crumpled flags hung from little windows.

'Mom thinks Armin might come back. Now that there's peace.'

I stopped crying. All of a sudden, everything became unimportant, as if the director had clapped his hands. I couldn't speak. It had been a long time since you last mentioned Armin, back in primary school. I was afraid I would say something stupid, something too pathetic, or not enough. It was our mission, which nobody else knew about. You pulled it out of your sleeve now, as a magic token during a difficult video game. I remembered his hands untying my ponytail years before. How he tilted his head to see me better, the same way you did when you found something interesting. How he held my hurt finger and said, *'Treasure Island.'* His face was getting lost in my memory, blurred, mixed with your own. It would come back to me each time I found myself in your room and saw his beach photo. But we never mentioned him, although he was the unbreakable connection between us, a secret calling which rendered everything else – Aleksandar, school, grades, first kisses – trivial.

'If your dad hears something . . .' you said, staring at the ground.

My dad. The one who decided we should observe *slava* all of a sudden. Mom went through newspapers looking for articles that explained how to celebrate the family patron saint faultlessly. Such infractions were unforgivable then – guests sat at our table like a jury ready to condemn the slightest mistake. Mom would forget to serve the oats. Dad would glance at her disappointedly, his lips pursed; he would have to scold her later.

The night he hit her, I ran out of the house in fear, as if the kitchen had suddenly filled up with rats that lived in the dark behind the fridge and the oven and whose existence I had been unaware of. I ran all the way to your front yard and threw tiny rocks at your window until you woke up and let me in. You accepted me into your circle, we were *the two of us* – no rodents could hurt us. Mom avoided me after that; she was more upset with me than she was with Dad. As if that night, with my elopement, I had taken something away from her; my own scene had deprived hers of meaning. The role of a suffering wife didn't shine as much in the shadow of a runaway daughter.

My dad. The one who, on my thirteenth birthday, took me to a church with his lame leg and paid the priest to baptize me. Mom wanted me to wear a white dress, but Dad wouldn't hear of it. 'Too conspicuous,' he said. The church was cold and empty, like a catacomb. The priest looked tired, he wanted to be somewhere else. It crossed my mind that maybe he'd spent the night there, in the silk habit, large and round like a fattened offering before the sad eyes of a colorful Christ. And I was too big under the priest's shaky hands and all his ritual props. I was wrong, although I had done nothing bad. He was frowning – my boatman to salvation, father's paid hand. His fat belly touched my elbow. My hair was wet on our way back home and I was cold. But Dad held my arm proudly and walked down the Alley as if he had won me in a competition.

My dad. The one who said, 'Six months and you close the case,' and I thought, for the first time in my life, that I could stab him in the neck with the duck bone. Him – who always took my side, not Mom's. He said it just like that, between two bites, turning Armin and everything he ever was into a case someone closed. A folder in the bottom drawer.

My dad. The one who will die in his sleep one day, although I didn't know it yet. He will stop, peaceful like a well-fed puppy, without a sound, with a smile on his face. I will be in Dublin, rejecting Mom's calls because my friends had come over for Scrabble. I will call her the next day and lie. 'I left my cell phone at work.' Her crying voice will tell me that Dad died, sounding surprised, as if expecting me to change her mind. And my first, unstoppable thought – it isn't fair. He should have suffered a bit.

I won't go to the funeral, I will miss the plane. I will persuade myself that it wasn't on purpose. She will hate me for it, for all the neighbors and police wives who will ask, 'Where's Sara?' and she will have to lie and invent excuses. I will feel guilty, yet stubbornly remind myself of that one sentence in order to feel better – 'Six months and you close the case.'

My dad. If my dad heard something. You said this as if worried that you were asking too much. And I answered, 'Sure.'

I never asked him anything. I don't know why. Some days went by, some weeks. Peace was no longer news. Electricity came back for good, I could stay up longer. Aleksandar never crossed my mind. I came to school each morning, expecting to see you altered, so I would instantly know, without a word, that your brother had returned. But this never happened. Armin went back to being the one we didn't talk about, the one whose existence was taken at face value, but never mentioned, like air.

We got a new math teacher, just like that, no explanations offered. I secretly hoped that you would be Lejla again, that I would be able to call you by your real name, now that the peace treaty had been signed. But after so many years, you let Lela Berić take over without a fight. The little *j* in your name belonged to me only. I didn't want to share it with other people. You had always been Lela to them; it was too complicated to change your name back and forth. Besides, it didn't matter to you. You no longer found yourself in a handful of letters. The way those people who often move house tend to lose their sense of home.

I remember the piece of paper hanging on the entrance to the Faculty of Philosophy, with the list of students admitted to Serbian Language and Literature. I remember reading *Lela Berić*, thinking how this nonexistent freak had cheated you out of a whole life, had taken everything from you: the math teacher, your first sex, your college admission.]

eight

I parked in Lejla's street and decided to walk to the town center. My phone was still out of battery so I had nothing to light my way. I walked slowly, feeling with my fingers the rusty ribs of someone's fence by my side, afraid I would fall into a hole in the ground where no one would find me.

The darkness was different. Different from the pale dusk in Mostar or the bluish night of Jajce. There was a thickness to it which mixed with the air so that I was surrounded not by a lack of light, but with a living, tangible substance. I felt like I was breathing it in, that it had become entangled with all the other smells: the smoke descending from the nearby hills, the weeds sprouting out of the deformed pavement, the stench of the far-away river.

I dreaded what those dark particles would do to me once they had filled my lungs and passed into my bloodstream. My veins had been clean for far too long, they wouldn't know how to react.

I walked squinting, trying to see what lay ahead. Somewhere in the distance, downtown, weak lights were visible,

foggy dots scattered throughout the black, like a photo nega-
tive of the moles on Lejla's back.

I touched the edges of my town with my fingertips: wild
hedges with thorns here and there, wire fences with sharp
leaves breaking through them, the dried-up bark of some
trees, dumpsters in the depths of which something moved,
crumpling and fidgeting. Some small life better equipped for
the darkness than I was.

This is where it starts, I thought. We had reached the
bottom. I was certain that a spring lay somewhere, the source
from which all that darkness poured out as a thick mass
and spread across what used to be my town, and hers, and
Armin's. How would I find Ranko? I would look for his stone-
cold lips with my fingers.

I wanted to go back to Lejla's street and wait for her in
the car.

The vehicle suddenly seemed familiar, something alive
and mobile in all the mute darkness. I could use it like one of
those transparent vessels used to explore the bottom of the
ocean, where everything is desolate and deaf-mute; where
you might come across the skeleton of an unfortunate ship
if you're lucky. But I only had two legs and two palms with
which to feel the wasteland, and a nose and ears to warn me
about the fiends that loomed out of decrepit, weed-ridden
backyards. It wasn't until I reached the municipal park that
my eyes were somewhat used to darkness. I was finally able
to make out familiar silhouettes. Here and there a streetlamp
flickered feebly, like a shy girl in a nightclub. Frightened light
bounced off a large human shape – a monument to that
forgotten writer forever carrying stone books in his hands.

Petar Kočić. When I came closer to him, I realized he had lost his books – someone had knocked his arms off and left two stumps gaping crudely in the air, unfinished. A metallic flicker revealed the line of the crooked clock that memorialized the great earthquake of 1969. A long time ago, coming back from a rather sad Night of Museums, I saw a man kicking his wife in front of that clock. We were all just standing, watching, waiting for someone else to do something. When he was done, he disappeared from the Square, and the poor woman stood up and headed in the direction of the market. First she straightened her skirt with her hands. The clock maintained its silence. As did the people.

There was nobody in the Square now, or at least I couldn't see anyone in the dusk. Pale posters danced in midair, like tired ghosts, covering the never-completed hotel building. Someone walked right by me in that moment, a slow, minuscule person, so close to me that I jumped out of fear. After this, I noticed a second, and a third. They moved stealthily, in all directions, like chess pieces without a board. They had always been there, yet so slowed that I hadn't sensed them in the dark. At first I thought I was surrounded by children – I couldn't see their faces, but they seemed strangely short next to me. However, there was not a trace of childhood in their movements – they walked heavily and with great pain, as if pulling beached ships behind them. I realized then that they were all elderly. Deep sighs and a barely visible reflection of white heads gave them away.

An army of old men and women surrounded me. Their spines were curved almost to the ground. Some of them stopped when they noticed me, obviously better accustomed to the darkness than I was. Under the only light bulb, which hung from the old department store building like an execution, an old woman smiled at me and then crossed herself in wonder, as if she had seen a relative long dead and gone. The youngest faces I encountered that night were the ones printed on the ripped election posters from a different era, covering the facade in the main street.

Downtown, light came from a window here and there, which helped me find the backyard of my house. But what I saw was a tombstone of a home overgrown by weeds, chipped and forgotten. The old pine, under which I had buried my three turtles so many years ago, was gone. They were cold in my hand, their necks unnaturally extended and exposed, outside the shell. Mom and Dad didn't know I buried them there. They feared some dog would dig them out so they told me to place them in a plastic bag and toss them in a dumpster. I couldn't imagine that. My turtles deserved better. Although it was *my* fault, Mom explained. I didn't feed them properly, I didn't clean their aquarium regularly, it was my responsibility, not hers. I can still remember their cold weight on my palms and how I thought that this was death, that *I* had done it. I buried them deep in the ground, my knees were dirty later, my nails too. But there was comfort in the pine tree. It had been there for my whole childhood, an undisputable and safe thing, a silent witness to my turtles. It would exist long after I was gone and remember my sin. It would carry it on its strong, barky back.

I was standing at the corner now, staring at the pointless space, which had once been filled with pine branches. When did she cut it down? Probably after Dad died. Perhaps a parasite had attacked the trunk. I didn't know; I hadn't talked to my mom in years. It had probably never crossed her mind that I was someone who should be told the pine was felled.

If there was a part of me that had wanted to contact her, it went quiet after I saw that emptiness. It was no longer my backyard. That was no longer my house. I saw she had changed the front door, too – it was wider, with two big wooden wings as if a religious leader dwelled behind them. And then they opened, so abruptly that I hid behind the neighbor's oak and crouched in the rosebush afraid I would be seen.

An unknown thin woman with a long, crooked neck appeared from that house I had once called my own, where I had once done my homework with Lejla. A little light coming from inside helped me get a better view of her. She had cropped black hair and large, thick glasses on her broad nose. I had never seen her before – the woman who had just opened the door of *my* house, one wing first, then the other. She then returned inside as if she'd forgotten something there, something that needed such a big opening. Soon after she appeared walking backwards, pulling a heavy wheelchair in which my mother sat. At first I saw her swollen white ankles that had no trace of life in them, as if someone had pasted another person's flesh on my mother. A bloated belly lay where the knees were supposed to be, swallowing my mother like quicksand, turning her into a uniform shape, a pile of mass, with a lock of blonde hair on top of it and two small eyes under the frowning forehead. She was deformed, as if a giant toddler had taken her into his clumsy hands and disfigured her like Play-Doh. In that darkness, I searched her face for some trace of that woman who had once braided my hair so tightly that I could still remember the pain in my temples. I wanted to recall the mother who clipped my nails, got me ready for school, put an apple and a chocolate bar in my backpack, told me to take the main road home and not to jump over the fence so that everyone could see my knickers as if my father were a peasant, and not chief of police. I searched the ugly heap of fat for anything to do with me and my life, something I had come from, the way earthquake victims go back to their shattered houses looking for personal belongings and find nothing there, only dust and broken glass.

The tiny woman parked the wheelchair by the garden table and my mother, wiping the plastic tablecloth with her forefinger, screamed, 'Can't anything in this house be clean?!' Upon hearing this, the woman took a cloth out of her apron pocket and started wiping the table hurriedly, which my mother observed with disgust in her face.

'Would you like your lunch now, or . . .' the poor woman asked in quivering voice.

'And when should I want it? Tomorrow?'

The table was soon covered with food. I was standing behind the bush, watching my mother eat. Compared to the rest of her body, her hands looked small, her fingers stumped and pulpy, with shiny tips. She brought food to her tiny, pouting lips with tired dedication, no visible pleasure at sight. It was something to be done, a wearisome bureaucratic task – all the bread, and the meat, and the potatoes, and the pie, and who knows what else.

'Petka! Petka!' she shouted between two bites. And Petka

peeked through the window, the steam coming out from the next dish.

'Yes, ma'am?' she answered.

'Don't forget the fish. You burned it the last time.'

'Oh, nah, ma'am, I check it regularly, I'm preparin' the *baklava* now.'

'And cut their heads off. For the soup,' my mother added with half a potato in her mouth.

'Whatcha say, ma'am?'

'I say CUT THE HEADS OFF! You deaf?'

'Yes, yes, that's next . . .' the answer came from the kitchen.

I won't lie – when Lejla told me to stop *at home*, something in me thought that perhaps this was to be the day I would visit my mother, apologize for missing Dad's funeral, for not calling her more often. I used to imagine the scene – we would both cry, or I would at least; she would hug me, say something she'd never said before, changed with all the time and loss; she would smell of that sugary scent she used to buy together with body lotion and hair oil; she would make me coffee, ask about Michael. My pathetic scenario embarrassed me now that I was hiding in someone's roses, looking at my mother stuff herself with food. And then, just as I was trying to sneak out unnoticed, a thorn pricked me. I jerked my hand and the rustling of the bush reached her. She stopped eating and looked up in my direction, squinting without her glasses.

'Petka!' she shouted. 'Petka, there's someone in the roses!'

I started running as fast as I could, although Petka hadn't heard her, nor could she ever catch me, scrawny and small as she was. I ran through the dark streets, far from the freak in the wheelchair and her two tiny eyes pushed deep into the Play-Doh. I ran back to the town center, all the way to the heroes, thinking of cut-off fish heads floating in the big pot on my mother's stove. I hid behind the monument and, once I made sure no one was coming after me, I sat on one of its steps to get some air.

I wish I were one of those contemporary heroines who, usually at the start of the novel, inform us that they never cry. They say something along the lines of *I couldn't cry, although I wanted to*, or for instance *the last time I cried I was four*. And we think that's good, the writer has escaped sentimentality, she created a strong female character. But the truth is I was sitting on that monument, crying like a spoiled child, with my eyes, and my nose, and my mouth, and my shoulders, figuring I had enough time to dry my eyes, wipe my nose, and collect myself before Lejla arrived. I cried as if such crying would prove that something had once existed, some idea of home or family, a story I could tell Michael's friends over wine and canapés. I had expected something, just like Lejla had in the AVNOJ Museum. I have no idea what.

I couldn't see his face in the dark, but I knew which one of the heroes was Ranko Šipka, there, almost at the end of the circle. They all stared straight ahead, only his head turned slightly to the side. I needed that old, adolescent skill of finding something pathetic, inventing a cozy drama and pushing it to the center of my day like a coin in a cold bread cake. I lay on the monument and put my hands under my cheek, picturing Ranko, the young Yugoslav soldier, moving his eyebrows, pieces of stone scattering around his face as he blinks, one leg breaking through the cold marble block, then the other, like a child learning to walk again after the braces have been removed. He walks toward me, the monument-man, wiping little specks of stone and dust off his uniform, tall and straight, with his cap in his hands. He approaches me and asks me, 'Are you all right, comrade?' And I tell him about the pine tree and my turtles and my mother who is now as big as that sad country. And he, *Ranko Šipka, 1917 – 1944*, takes me into his arms, the way soldiers used to do in old movies, while Lejla's father is singing an old-time ballad; he takes me back to his bust, back to the monument he just stepped out of. He gets back into it, one leg becomes marble again, then the next, as my living, organic body gives in to the final rite without protest. His hands harden and I, held in them, and my mouth and my eyelids; everything I call myself dries up, stiffens, turns to stone. We stay there, forever the same, and he says, 'Shhh, it's all right now.' I could hear church bells ringing far away, the sound spread in slow circles, as if a care-less hand of a child had dropped a stone and disturbed our dirty puddle. And Ranko kept saying, 'Shhh, shhh . . .'

When I woke up, I saw Lejla's eyes. They were black again. She was lying by my side, looking at me.

'Are you insane?' she whispered. 'What do you think you're doing, sleeping on monuments like an idiot?'

'It's Ranko's fault,' I said. She could tell I'd been crying – she had sensors for everything human in me.

'What happened with the blue contacts?' I asked.

'Took them out before. 'Cause of Mom.'

'How's your mom?'

'Same as always,' she answered. 'Packed us some spinach pie.'

I lay on my back and looked at the sky, although I couldn't really tell the darkness above from the one that surrounded us. Everything was one, the sky had merged with Banja Luka, and Lejla and I were floating somewhere in midair, on the cold stone, neither up nor down.

'Sara,' she said eventually. 'Let's go.'

[The bus is quiet. We're sitting at the very back, again. Me on one side, you on the other, each one with her own window. A thick *Introduction to Linguistics* between us – the exam is in about ten days and we have learned nothing. Something is over, or has at least begun being over. I won't admit it yet.

We have spent almost all of August on the island, eating olives and burning in the sun. Now we're staring through the window at the landscape that is irrevocably transforming into something serious, continental, concrete.

The sand and the sea are gone. The bus is shivering and jumping over bumps as if a frightened animal has swallowed us. It's still hot. Dust rises from spongy seats with the stench of all the heads that had rested there.

Your legs are tanned and covered in red bites, which your nail has turned into little crosses. You stare through the window as if we are in open space and you're waiting for a planet or an unnamed star to appear. But there's nothing there. Only someone's little houses and someone's little lives. Each new threshold takes a bit of our summer away from us.

This is the last time I see your black hair, though I don't know it then. I want to talk to you, end the silence, but anything I could possibly say seems fake, precooked, and foreign. Words have failed me. If I could apologize to you in numbers, I would. But I don't know how to use mathematics purposefully. It's a different kind of cognition, aimed at those who see meaning outside of language, those minds that are direct and sharp like yours. As always, I go back to my stumbling words. I fidget. I say, '*Because death requires fantasy. Creative fantasy.*' You throw a tired glance at me, a you-gotta-be-kidding-me kind of look. But you have always been one of those people who respect the rules of the game even if they abhor the other players. You don't say anything, instead you just get up and move tiredly down the narrow aisle from the rear to the front of the bus. You check the seats, looking for the book I quoted among the pinch of readers. Then you get back to your seat, mutter, '*Ivan Galeb*,' pull your legs up, and close your eyes, crushing something in my stomach. I watch you pretend to be sleeping and I know. The unbreakable phrase, *Lejla and I*, cracked on that island. I did that, in the water, with one sentence.

Sooner or later, all buses reach their destination. We came back home and started sophomore year at college. I phoned you before the first class so that we could go together. Your mom said you weren't home.

'That's OK,' I answered, 'we'll meet there.'

But you weren't there. I entered the lecture theater and got a seat in the back. People came in, sat down, opened their textbooks, and sharpened their pencils. You were nowhere to be seen. The teacher appeared, too. She told us to sign our names on a piece of paper and let it circulate. It took a long time to reach me – I was in the last row. I signed next to my typed name and then, at the very top of the list, read *Lela Berić*. I saw your unintelligible, sharp signature in red ink. You were there, you had come to class. My eyes jumped from one head to the other, but I couldn't find you. We had sat together during freshman year. Dammit, we had been sitting together since elementary school and all through high school. And you were somewhere else now, with someone else. Someone who didn't know about Armin. Someone who didn't know about the sparrow. And all because of that damn island. I ruined everything.

'Miss, can you hand me the attendance list if everyone has signed?'

All those heads turn to me and, thanks to my myopia and your tricks, none of them is yours. I stand up and walk down the stairs as if to be slaughtered at the end of the road. I hand the sheet to the teacher and start heading back to my seat. And finally – I see you. You are sitting in the second row. Your hair is blonde. All that hair, from its root to your navel, is yellow and wrong. An insult to our entire friendship. Some guy whispers something into your ear. You laugh, not even looking at me as I walk past, laughing with that dumbass, you and your false hair, giggling like someone else, some stupid little girl who has never played chess or read Kiš. A poor thing with half a brain in her pretty head. Lela Berić.

I walk toward my place slowly, and feel an organ disappear inside me with each step. The teacher is talking about phonetics, a new, perfumed notebook is opened before me, but your head, framed with its shameless yellowness, keeps smudging my sight, irritating my eyes like sand. I sit and listen, empty and tired. Later I get up and walk home, rolling down the main street like a discarded can. There was no point in staying or saying anything. You explained it all with your hair and the idiot whispering in your ear, his meaty lips nearly touching your small earring.

I arrived home and threw up. My mom entered the bathroom, shut the door behind her, and hissed nervously, but silently, lest Dad should hear, 'Are you pregnant? I know you're pregnant!' From what? I almost asked. From Lejla, who died on the island, doesn't exist anymore? From fish and lobsters? Devious sea currents? But I just shook my head, washed my face, and went to my room. I realized in that moment that I had nobody to call to complain about Lela Berić. I was alone and ordinary, curled up on my bed like a side effect in my own bedroom. It was over. I undid our friendship. Nothing tied me to Armin any longer. The case was closed. What do convicts do on their first day out of prison? They feel fear. Unimaginable, monolithic fear before the 'sea of possibilities'. I think I realized that then, sitting on that bed, alone and ordinary and without a *j* in your name.

And then a day, then a week, then a month. Time became something I was acutely aware of – the external, imposed kind of time measured with clock hands and bells. I became aware of the length of a minute and an hour, my pulse matched the seconds. One day without *the two of us*. Two weeks without *the two of us*. A digital timer lay somewhere on my diaphragm, it started ticking the moment I saw your blonde hair in the second row of the lecture theater. My life split into a before and an after, as if I had survived a car accident or joined a hardline sect.

I tried to call you only once. Your mom said you weren't home, in a voice too gentle, as if apologizing for having to lie. And that evening, remember, when I bumped into you and some guy next to Safikada's grave? You had always loved that spot, ever since we were little. You had known about it long before the town administration decided to mark it. It wasn't the love story that fascinated you, or the mythical heroine, or all those candles left on that plain stone by women of Banja Luka, those who believed they would give meaning to their own story by celebrating someone else's. No, you thought all that was ridiculous. It was the *death* that fascinated you, something that had happened such a long time ago, but was still there, on that corner; a death not hidden in a graveyard, not framed with flowers and mourners, but right there, exposed in the middle of the city for everyone to see. Something so simple that an ignorant traveler would pass it by without a second glance, not knowing his coat had brushed a bit of this death, that it would catch up with him or her, sooner or later. But that evening you were there by accident, accompanied by the guy of the week. You were drunk. You ran into me and burst out laughing. I was shamefully sober for a Saturday. You looked at me condescendingly, as if I had reminded you of everything you had decided to forget about yourself, things that no longer had the right to consider themselves yours. The guy, I can't remember which one – there were so many back then – saw me and said, 'Look, it's our pretty classmate . . .' or something similar. And you gave him that new giggle you had composed in the last month as a slap in the face to our whole story. You pulled him by the sleeve and that was it. I was left alone next to Safikada, next to death. A candle was crooked, dripping on the ground, the wax made a little bridge from the wick to the stone. I tried to straighten it, but only managed to break it. I left it like that, mutilated and extinguished, next to the others. After all, who was I to straighten other people's candles, to fix other people's clichés? It crossed my mind that you were right – nobody in their right mind should hang out with me.

On the second floor of the Faculty of Philosophy some-one had written in permanent marker, *'For all have felt the breeze / and Lela on her knees.'* I took a key from my purse and scratched your name off the wall. I looked after you even in those places: in the filthy toilets, amidst someone's piss and used condoms. I looked after you although you weren't talking to me and the accidental iambic trimeter on that wall probably spoke the truth. I didn't need your gratitude; you never had to find out. I did it for myself, to have a small calling, a sense of self-appreciation for being fair, for acting as your anonymous toilet hero on the second floor. In the meantime you spread your legs under every pimply moron from our year. When you were done, you moved on to seniors.

I shared a desk with three girls. Each one of them had a curse on her face: a big nose, a big forehead, a big set of teeth. They spoke in a vicious chorus, gossiping their hissing whispers over one another, fixing the victim with their gaze, which was you most of the time. 'Look at her, what a slut, you can see cocks in her eyes,' they would say. 'What kind of scum do they allow into university nowadays . . .' or 'skin and bone 'cause of all the fucking' and other similarly uninventive mantras used to turn themselves, if only for a moment, into something different, something pure and beautiful, something which wasn't Lela Berić. I would change the subject, ask about a textbook or consulting hours, interrupt them, not because I minded their cursing, but only to stop hearing that name. They would turn to me abruptly, the three-headed six-eyed monster, angry because I upset the sorcery. They read your behavior as a biblical story of a fallen woman who had once been virtuous. But I knew the truth. There was no innocence lost, no falling into sin. This was Lejla, spreading Lela's legs, pimping her, dragging her by the hair down the road. You wanted to stretch your fake name between all those guys until it split apart, until it was drawn through the gutter so many times that the only thing left for it was to die, alone and worn out, a drunkard under a bridge. Then, maybe, you would be able to shed your second skin, once it was dead and dry enough. Your black mane would grow back. You would be *you* again. I believed this once or at least wanted to. But then, years later, I saw you standing in front of that restaurant in Mostar, you and your white hair, and realized I had been wrong. You took all the color out of your hair, and got into a white car. The little viper had shed all of its many skins without ever growing a new one. It had rejected the shell because it was more painful than sunlight.

You dragged Lela's name around toilets. I dragged Sara's around literary magazines. In the end, isn't that the same thing? I started writing after you had dyed your hair blonde. I needed to have something under my control, to be a god of certain small worlds. I invented heroines with legs stronger than mine, who didn't burst into tears at every little thing, who delivered smart, informed answers in a language I never used. I invented half-men, half-freaks, who had no basis in reality, invented their little hobbies – collecting butterflies for instance – and sent them off on impossible routes where they would lose everything. I would degrade them to their lowest limit, to breaking point, and they would still manage to wiggle out in the last sentence. I would save their miserable lives; I would be their faceless goddess of mercy. One night I went so far that I invented an entire dark-haired man, whose shirts smelled of lemon, who carried an HB pencil in his pocket and had a scar on his cheek. I invented the books in his hands and his fingers smudged with graphite, and the sidewalks under his shoes. I wrote him an impossible itinerary that would lead to my bed until one night I simply killed him off in two sentences. I invented stories, stupid, illogical stories that made our town sound like a magical Scandinavian countryside where no darkness ever dwelled, where people never disappeared, and my heroines could bathe in the river like in a Jacuzzi. None of this made any sense, but I didn't really care – as long as one word followed the other, there was no point in stopping and considering the question of responsibility. Sometimes the stories were short, unfinished, and untold, and I would cut them up into verses and turn them into bad poems. I wrote too fast, without thinking, in a notebook intended for math. I never liked lines. I wrote shameful words where your superior numbers should have been. I stuffed the little squares like peppers. I sent them everywhere, wherever there was a literary review, leftist, rightist, student, academic, from the very center of a metropolis to the most provincial corner – I didn't care. I thought that one of them would reach our university, one way or another, reach the college library. One of my stories or poems would get to you, whether you wanted it or not. You would have to read it under my stupid, monolithic name. You would have to listen to me. And if I wrote something truly valuable, truly good, in a little language that lies under a ton of washed-out, false words, perhaps I could reach Armin too.

But you consistently ignored all of that, my poems bounced off you the way bullets bounce off armored vehicles. You showed up at the launch of my poetry collection. My dad had hired a string quartet and paid a scrawny actress to read my lines. The whole circus without sense or reason – you glanced at it with contempt, I could see your eyes in the last row.

You came with a guy, you dragged them around like crutches back then, and I was embarrassed by my weak, false verse dropping out of the overrated actress. I saw disgust in your face, something that had been waiting to surface ever since that winter morning when I killed the sparrow. Copies of my book were lined up on the table. You gave them a look full of pity, as if they were dead birds I had stepped on as well. And I know what you were thinking: that I had sold them a nonexistent story, that I had washed my hands clean of all my crimes, that only you knew the real me – the one I had left out of the pages. You, Lela Berić, the woman sung in toilet verse by Banja Luka scumbags, passed from hand to hand like a baton in a relay race, you judged *me* and my clean, literary crime. I vomited a whole language for nothing, wasted it on fiction, while your beautiful brother still stood in your back-yard, under the cherry tree. We had outgrown him. I saw all of that in your eyes. And then you pulled the guy's sleeve and left my launch before the strings started squealing a dragged-out Bach.]

nine

'I gotta pee,' she announced and started going through her bag. I pretended I hadn't heard and looked in the rear-view as if to consider an important driving problem. We were in the middle of nowhere: all around us just uniform asphalt. As we got away from Banja Luka, the darkness became looser, less heavy on the pupils. I could see houses, scattered and tiny, like rocks knocked off a cliff. I could see dry flowers in strangers' backyards. I could see giving up. Not much road was left to get to the border. Each pore on my sweaty skin could sense that we were driving towards the exit, like a drowning person who finally figured out the surface was this way and the bottom the other. Half an hour and Bosnia would be behind us.

'Hello? Hear what I said?' Lejla asked and punched my shoulder.

'I can't stop here.'

'Well, you have to. I'm down to a drop.'

Down to a drop. She had to be the only person who used that. We are stacking up mats after a PE class. 'Sara, I'm down to a drop,' says Lejla and lets me finish the work. We're

sitting in that terrible concert, college graduation. 'I'm down
to a drop,' says Lejla, to everyone and no one, and gets up in
the middle of Tchaikovsky, urging a line of graduates to get
up and let her through.

'Hold it,' I said, though I also felt I was *down to a drop*. I
could feel her judgmental look. She knew I was dying to get
us out of the dark and, if necessary, would leave Bosnia in
pissed pants.

'Sara, please. I really have to pee.'

'Almost there.'

'Sara, for fuck's sake . . .'

'I'm not stopping the car.'

And then everything happened fast, faster than I would
admit – her skinny hand on the steering wheel stronger than
mine, the Astra following her sudden move like a scared
beast, my head bumping hard against the door, a cornfield
on the right, leaves slapping our car like insulted ladies, foot
on the brake. Stop. Everything around us was embarrassingly
dense and alive.

'What the fuck is wrong with you?! You can't do that!' I
yelled, but she got out and slammed the door. I shouted her
name in outrage but it only echoed bluntly and evaporated in
the dark, too frail to stop her long legs.

I could see her silhouette moving through slim stalks. It
looked like this wasn't the first time she had vandalized a
cornfield, as if all the agriculture of the world belonged to
her. The monotonous flora swallowed her up before I could
protest.

I checked my bloody head in the rearview. A small wound,
but painful. I couldn't hide it under my bangs; they were

too short. Damned deranged Lejla. Could nobody else in the whole wide world drive her to Vienna? Damned Vienna that seemed so far from the cornfield that it must be made up. Couldn't Dino drive her? Was he somehow disabled? His knees looked quite fine when I saw him. Perhaps he was an ex-convict, couldn't travel, on probation for robbing a kiosk. As if she ever cared whether or not I would see Armin. She could have used anyone else and never called me, it would have made no difference to her. I would have lived my life in blissful happiness, next to my naked neighbor, with my avocado tree. Instead, my head was bleeding at the edge of Bosnia, lucky I hadn't broken my neck, all because Lejla Begić had to take a piss.

I got out of the car, fighting the sharp greenery. Regardless of the dark, it was unbearably hot. I was trying to figure what to say to a curious driver when he or she pulled over to see our accident. What would I tell the police? What would I tell Michael? Though it was highly unlikely he would ever find out – my phone had been dead since AVNOJ.

A deer. I would say a deer ran in front of the car, I freaked out and made a sharp turn. Were there any deer there? I couldn't google my lie.

I looked in the direction Lejla had gone. I couldn't see her. The world was broken up into a hundred green cranes. I knew she was crouching there somewhere. Pretending that what she had done was completely normal. Perhaps it would have been normal if this was a different era and we were those two girls by the river. But not like this. Even she knew that this was not OK. We are no longer this, we no longer do such nonsense. She could have seriously hurt both of us. Had it all been a show to prove to me – the boring, adult me – how lame I was, how changed, while she stayed the same?

I walked through the corn, pushing tall stalks like people at a concert. I couldn't see her. The plants just snapped back and slapped my spine and face. I was the one disturbing their simple verticality. Was I walking in a straight line or had I taken a turn at some point? What if I was walking in a circle? Impossible, I had only taken a few steps. The Astra was still behind me, white in the dark, in the middle of the green, like the skeleton of a sunken ship. I kept walking and cursing. I stepped into wet, sticky earth. She was there, a wildling, making me follow her primitive trail like a puppy. Where had she gone? Perhaps if I laughed out loud, showed her I got the joke, no hard feelings. Completely normal. Then I could murder her later.

I realized I had to pee myself; the crime would have to wait. It took some strength to peel the jeans off my sweaty thighs. A plant stuck to my ass. I had forgotten how hot Bosnia was. Bosnia eaten by darkness, ridden with old age – I pissed on it. And where was Lejla? I could hear her steps rustling in the distance. I wiped myself with a dry leaf and pulled up my jeans. That's when I realized the field had tricked me – there was no life there. It was dead, all that corn, down to the last stalk. The heat dried their essence, crippled their slim leaves. The darkness took their color. We were in the middle of a corn cemetery, a field left by the road to die, forgotten.

In my ears, Lejla kept walking; I could hear her sneakers tapping the dry land and the dead growth slapping her naked shoulders. I no longer knew which direction I had come from, where the car was, where she was.

I started moving fast through the corn, one way, then another, and another, to no avail. The field seemed to be endless, stretching in all directions.

I turned around but could no longer see the car. I wanted to scream, perhaps Lejla could hear me, but I was afraid we might not be alone. Perhaps, a long time ago, other women had gotten lost in the same cornfield; the final cursed labyrinth for spiteful Bosnian girls before they reached the border. It was our little country, our piss-drenched anchor, telling us, 'Not so fast, where do you think you're going?' Did they die there, all those women craving exile, among those dried-up stalks, one step away from salvation? Did their bones turn to dust, mixed up with the earth Lejla and I pissed on?

It was hot and I was starving. Dull pain pulsated in my forehead. I sat down on the ground so I wouldn't faint. The barren earth would swallow me whole if I lost consciousness. I reminded myself of the plan. We would cross the border and drag ourselves to Zagreb, one way or another. I could take a shower then, have dinner and sleep, before moving on to Austria. It's only been a couple of days. A couple more and I'd be back with Michael. The thought calmed me. I thought it was all OK, everything was going on as planned, so perfectly that I could even lie down and take a little nap, hidden in that field. I would be safe, no one would find me.

I lay on the ground, all of a sudden immensely tired. I needed a break – from the dark, from driving, from Lejla. And then I heard her steps. She was getting closer. She was able to find me in the dark; the way sharks can smell blood from miles away. The corn stalks suddenly turned into flimsy stems. I saw her thin figure above me, white hair falling, almost reaching my face. She had undone the braid.

She pushed away an annoying stalk and sat down. She reached for my feet to lift them onto her lap, but I shook her off so violently that I accidentally kicked her elbow. I didn't really care. Let her hurt.

'Lejla, what the hell's wrong with you?' I said and got up.

'What the hell is wrong with *you*? I told you I had to pee.'

'You could have killed us!'

'*Killed us?* Don't be ridiculous, we literally only just left the road.'

'No, seriously. You can't do this. It's not OK. The car almost turned over.'

She let out a loud breath and lay on the ground.

'OK, whatever. You know what I just thought of?' she asked and then immediately answered her own question, 'Remember Maja from class 4B?'

'I don't give a shit about Maja from class 4B. First the whole show with the English at that Knežević woman's, now this crap. I'm tired of your bullshit.'

'My bullshit? Is that a nice little European talking now?'

'Fuck you, Lejla.'

'No, *fuck you, Lejla* no. I asked for a favor, you said yes. And now I'm supposed to be nice and polite, have the kind of hair you would like, wear the kind of clothes you would like, talk about what *you* want to talk about, tell you how *beautiful* our prom night was, forget I have bowels and a working bladder . . .'

'What is that supposed to mean?'

'It's like you forgot everything, Sara. You're blind.'

'I'm not blind, I'm a grownup.'

'Oh, yeah? Then tell me why I have a flip Motorola phone then.'

'The hell should I know?'

'You found it funny,' she said calmly. 'You think people choose everything in their lives. Because you have spent your whole life choosing everything. I have a fucking flip phone because it's the only one I could afford. I am a waitress because it was the only job I could get. And I am here now, because it seemed like the last option. So if you are uncomfortable, or bored, or angry, I sincerely apologize. But I'm not gonna be some nice little European *childhood friend* just because you seem to have forgotten who I really am.'

She said all of this without raising her voice once. Spread out on the ground among the dead corn she looked like an abandoned pet someone had thrown out the window in the middle of the night. I didn't know what to say. She always knew how to drive me out of sensible arguments, even when we both knew I was right. She would deliver a calm speech, lower it down around me like a cage, and let me fidget inside with my utterly useless wrath. She knew I didn't want to walk away. My wish to see Armin was obvious all over me, she could smell it with her beastly nostrils.

'I just wanna get to Vienna in one piece,' I said and sat down again.

I turned my back to her, ashamed by the futility of my anger.

'*I wanna get.* What about me? Are you driving me too? Or

is this *Sara's journey*? Sara *wants to get*. Our heroine will reach
the end of the road. In one piece.'

'Lejla, cut the crap. I'm obviously driving both of us.
You're the reason I'm here. OK?'

She was quiet. She had taken my anger, stripped it naked,
carved and remodeled it, and then reused it against me. She
was the master of spinning a situation. For someone who
could chit-chat for hours, she had the heaviest silence in the
world. It filled my ears like a poisoned sea. I lay back down
and took a deep breath of the dead field.

'So what about Maja from class 4B?' I asked after a while,
just to keep talking. I wanted to get out of the corn and continue the trip.

'Oh, Maja . . . You know . . . The one that allegedly put corn
sticks up her . . .'

'And you trust stupid Dejan,' I answered, annoyed; as if it
had been Dejan's fault we almost died.

'I trust neither Maja nor Dejan.'

'So what about it now? What's the point?'

'There's no point, Sara. You and your god damn points.'

'What's that supposed to mean?'

'Nothing,' she said.

'No, seriously. What do you mean, *me and my god damn
points*?'

'Well, the whole thing . . . Theme, motive . . . Setting. Not
everything has a point. Grow up.'

'*I* should grow up? You almost killed us because you had
to pee.'

'I didn't almost kill us . . . See? You're doing it again.'

'Doing what?'

'Inventing things. *You almost killed us.* We just left the road. We're completely fine. Is your life really that boring that you have to come up with some drama all the time?'

'Lejla, my forehead is bleeding.'

'I've been bleeding for three days and you don't see me whining about it.'

I didn't want to argue. I closed my eyes, massaged my temples, and tried to imagine we were somewhere else. On the island, perhaps. Before everything fell apart. I could smell the odor of dead corn and the burnt earth where Lejla had left her blood. I pictured a tiny, tired root reviving amidst the barren land, stubbornly fidgeting and sprouting, in spite of everything. I pictured her blood penetrating deep down into the dry earth and resurrecting the whole field. The corn stalks are golden and straight again.

I remembered we were close to the border. We were lying, two dots on a map, so very close to the red line. There was something comforting in that. I tried to picture Armin, older, gray-haired, looking at me in wonder after all those years, smiling – but I couldn't. Maja from class 4B came to my mind and the photo of her I saw on Facebook: she was in a wheelchair, wearing a heavy flower-patterned sweater, and her fat husband stood behind her, smiling. A son on each side, third one on her lap. Tired Maja from class 4B, proudly photographed for her five hundred virtual friends.

'Can I tell you a story?' Lejla asked me all of a sudden.

'Make sure it has no *point*, please. Since we're so *grown up*.'

'Of course there's no point.'

'What about theme and motive? Setting?'

'Theme: pedophilia. Setting: math class. There's no motive. Motives are as dumb as points.'

I got up on my elbows and looked at her. She was lying with her eyes closed, her pants still unzipped, her hand on her naked belly. Now and then a car drove by, lights flew over the horizon and then disappeared in the darkness.

'What do you mean, pedophilia? What are you talking about?'

'Math teacher. Remember? *My guy?*'

'What about him?'

'He attacked me . . . Actually, *attacked* is a stupid word. He jumped at me.'

'What?'

'What you heard.'

'When?' I asked.

'Sophomore year. I mean . . . I went to him, you know? I wanted to . . . I don't know. I have no idea why I went. And then he started groping me and his face turned all . . . beastly. Like a rabid dog.'

Her voice was calm, as if she was explaining a simple mathematical problem, half amused with my ignorance.

'So what happened?'

'Nothing. I pushed him and went out.'

'I can't believe this. So that's why he left, the bastard . . .'

'I think it was worse for him than for me. You should have seen the poor guy's face.'

'Lejla, you should have told someone. This is not OK. You were a minor.'

'Tell who? Nothing happened anyway.'

'It doesn't matter if nothing happened, the point is . . .'

'Here she goes again with the fucking point.'

'I'm just saying you should have reported him.'

She opened her eyes, took a deep breath, and sat up to look at me.

'Sara, you're exaggerating . . . He was younger than you and I are now.'

'That's completely irrelevant. You were a minor, he was your teacher.'

'Oh, cut the crap . . . You're only upset because you didn't know.'

I got up and headed towards the sound of cars. I couldn't stand her. She was full of herself, privileged and untouchable in her big knowledge.

'Sara, wait . . .'

'I don't wanna wait. I wanna get out of this fucking country as soon as possible.'

She ran up to me and took my hand. 'Wait, for fuck's sake . . .'

'Wait for what?' I asked. 'First you nearly kill us and then you tell me it's normal for some thirty-year-old moron to grope minors in his class?'

'The world is not that simple, Sara. Some people are just . . .'

'Just what? Pedophiles?'

'Lonely. Some people are just lonely.'

I sneered and kept walking towards the road. I could soon see the car where we had left it, white and wrong off the asphalt. I realized I would have to stop another driver and ask for help getting us out. I got up on the road and started to wave. A couple of cars honked and drove past me, I must have looked like a disheveled troll who lived in the cornfield and came out on the road every now and then to scare drivers.

'What do you think you're doing?' she asked.

'What do *you* think I'm doing? Someone's gonna have to pull us out. Because you had to pee.'

'No one's gonna stop this way. You're jumping around like an idiot.'

Lejla climbed up to the street and stretched her long, tanned arm with a thumb-up. Two or three cars later, a small Peugeot pulled over and drove in reverse to where we were.

'Now it's gonna be some maniac. We're gonna end up in someone's basement, without kidneys. Because you had to piss.'

'There's your story,' she answered.

An elderly woman got out of the car, wearing jeans and a shirt in bright colors. Her hair had that special purple hue of giving up. Lejla started explaining the situation, with a Lela Berić smile and an I-have-a-major-in-Serbian-literature accent. She failed to mention the part about her hand on the steering wheel.

'I see . . . I see . . .' the woman said, glancing at the Astra. She waved her hand and started walking back to her car. For a moment I thought she would abandon us, we would spend the night in the cornfield. But she came back, half-irritated, carrying a tow strap, as if this wasn't the first time she was pulling lost girls out of the corn.

'Come on, girls . . .' she said, handed me the iron hook and walked back to her car. A long black strap unwound between us. When she got to her Peugeot, she turned back and shouted, 'Pull up your sleeves and get down to business. This ain't a disco.'

[I have to tell that story too. Pull up my sleeves. None of this has any point without it. Although you refuse to see points. But there aren't many memories left in my frozen lake. A crack here and there, soon it's all gonna be dead chunks of crystal. Mrs. Knežević will carve a little duck and add it to the cupboard. Don't overestimate your own importance. This is just my tired fingers wringing out an old piece of cloth. Soon I'll go dry, like the cornfield. Until then, let's go on.

Look – one crack. The island, that summer before the end of the world. Warm sea and cold beer. Look – you can see it better now.

The place where we stopped being *you and me*; where your hair was black for the last time. Let's tell this story, too. I won't look for a point, I promise.

I will hide it somewhere in your ear so nobody can find it. Have you noticed I never described your ears? There you go. They won't know where to look.

For example, let's start at the beach. The beach is long and full of loud children. Hysterical mothers catch them around the sand, take shells out of their mouths, frantically apply greasy sunscreen over their small, smooth backs. Fathers lie in the shade and check your round ass every time you walk to the water to refresh your feet. We've just finished freshman year at college and think we're the smartest people in the world. We are certain that we're mature, that being intelligent means getting a ten and being able to quote Miljković. We glance at the worried mothers condescendingly, over the edge of our dark sunglasses. From here, far away, I can see how naïve, how unequal we are to those real, fatigued women. I can see our tight skin and firm breasts, our hot brains only recently completed, our unexplained hunger for that something, that *other*, which would never come. And the absolute certainty that we would never be like them – ordinary people – that our hair would never fall lifelessly over our peeling shoulders the way it did on the plump women who ran after their brats on the scorching sand. How much of that superior delusion can fit into one moment at the beach? But I can't leave anything out, though I can barely remember a thing except you and that morning. I have to recall a generic beach, describe sand that smells like postcard-sand, and the sun round and shiny as if Photoshopped. I have to invent an olive tree and mosquitos and get all the senses working, right? Then the story is *believable*. I should describe the smells (sea salt, the sweat of tanned boys pressing against us in the disco and your coconut shampoo), the taste (olives, watermelons, vodka which is never cold enough, blueberries; you tasted my eye that night something got in it); the sounds (birds, I'll get an ornithology handbook and will name each and every one; I'll write smart sentences); the visible (our legs, our lips, our hands, only us, nothing else was worthy of our youthful conceit); the touch (my eyeball with your tongue, your hair in the sea, looking for your face in all that blackness). The senses, use all the senses. As if the story would be *alive* then. You hate all these pompous attempts to make something dead look alive. And here I go stumbling after that same primitive trace. Don't get angry. Someone has to tell this too, even if it's me.

We read in a magazine that some people were getting ready for the end of the world. They said everything would just disappear in the year 2000. Some mentioned Armageddon, an unprecedented meteor shower that would obliterate the human race. Others talked of the great flood: cars, rooftops, cattle, they'll all be floating on the surface of a murky puddle. We read about people who gave away everything they owned, gave up their homes, abandoned their mortgages and permanent contracts, ready to meet the end of everything; the end of themselves. This was *the last summer*, your final opportunity to wear your red swimsuit that tied around the neck and learn how to dive headfirst, before the world stopped. Our parents accepted the joke as long as we spent the month preparing for the exams that we failed to pass last year. But there was something in us that half believed the world really would end. What if this was the last time sea salt bit our skin? The end of the world didn't scare me; it was too exaggerated to be true. I was afraid of the end of *us*.

But let me describe you a bit. To make them drool, you'd like that.

Me – so ordinary next to you, wearing my black swimsuit like the certificate of lost virginity. I iron my hair in vain, trying to copy your ease and the way you eat juicy watermelon slices. Salty drops gather timidly on your skin, your smile is perfectly crooked, a smooth black ponytail relaxing on your shoulder, glimmering in sun and water like a young raven's plumage.

I spend whole mornings waiting for you to wake up. You always needed more sleep than an average human. We massage olive oil into our skin and walk to the sea steadily, like newly hatched sea turtles returning home. Everyone looks at you as you pull the summer dress over your head, in one quick move, like an annoying bandage. Everyone looks at you as you spread the orange towel the size of someone's living room and they quietly accept your right to the largest territory. Everyone looks at you as you enter the sea, your step doesn't falter when air turns to water, you go on in the same rhythm, while a bunch of mortals around you test the temperature in hasty unbecoming moves, like toys about to run out of battery. Everyone looks at you, and I look at them; I'm both envious and proud, wanting to tell them, 'That's enough now.'

There's nothing special about you. The beach is full of longer legs, bigger breasts, and other, equally overrated miracles of human symmetry. But you carry a promise of a different world, a uniqueness that all those average beggars crave. You carry a story. That's what everyone wants, right? Someone to give them a theme, a motive, a setting? The beginning and the end. A point. That's why you hate them.

What really happened on that island? I've told myself the story a hundred times, I started telling it the moment I saw your blonde hair in the lecture room and realized we were no longer anything. I kept looking for some meaning in what happened. But *what* happened? Water, all that water, which is no longer part of the beach, but belongs to the sea and the ocean. Your hair, your red swimsuit, the bow on the back of your neck.

No, wait a minute. Not so fast. We'll get there. Let me write a couple of leisurely seaside days, while we're sitting on the floor of that little room in the ugly hotel whose facade has been peeling off since socialism. We've got a bottle of gin and blueberry juice. We were trying to roll a joint. I coughed, you laughed – it was the first time. The only luxury item in our room was an enormous radio set probably from back in the day when Tito came to cut the red ribbon at the opening ceremony. From the few buzzing channels, we managed to catch one with classic oldies. You rolled a turban around your head and imitated Olivera Marković singing '*your little mouth-harmonica which plays for me only . . .*' and I was cracking up, because of you and the weed. '*And my heart goes dum dum . . . And my heart goes dom dom . . .*' sang the drunk, black-haired Olivera, tone-deaf, next to my paralysis. '*And I would reach out to you . . .*' She gave me your hands.

'I'm gonna fall,' I said and started laughing again. But you pulled me closer anyway. I couldn't dance and just put my hands on your shoulders like a blind person would.

'Can you tell I'm stoned?' you asked me. I looked into your eyes, they were as black as usual; I could never see your pupils anyway. But I said, 'Yes, I can definitely tell,' because I knew that's what you wanted to hear.

Milan Timotić sang after Olivera. He told us that a journey to *a big city* is awaiting us who *dream of happiness*. We believed him. You took a deep breath, pulled me closer, and kept dancing. You whispered, 'Dad used to sing this . . . *You're not the first soul dreaming of happiness now . . .'* You didn't get a single tone right, but that didn't matter, your lack of musicality was soothing. Alcohol and pot mixed in my head. I could hear a different era, in some town where *a life always new streams on uninterrupted,* while your father sings on in his immaculate tenor voice, and our grandmothers wear pastel-colored dresses and dance on heels so high they would sprain our ankles. There was no darkness, the island embraced us in its naïve carelessness, and the sea salt ate our memory. I almost believed, there in the hotel room, half-drunk and half-stoned, in some silly story about a happier time where spotted skirts swirled and wheat fields waved and little stars glimmered on blue hats. I know what you're going to ask if you read this. I don't know why I did it, Lejla. No idea. Perhaps because I believed, perhaps because it seemed logical, perhaps because I imagined you were someone else, someone who looked like you. It wasn't a real kiss really; I barely touched your lips. I wanted to prove something, maybe that I was cool and could kiss anyone I liked. But you broke into intoxicated laughter, gently pushed me away and said, 'You can't do that in Bosnia.'

'We're not in Bosnia,' I answered. Not because I wanted to kiss you again, but because I wouldn't let you lead. But you just looked at me as if I were a child and said, 'We're always in Bosnia.'

I can't remember whether we said anything else. That same night we were busy kissing local boys in a little disco that smelled of dust and sweat. I looked at other girls and tested my desires. I realized I wasn't attracted to any of them.

I didn't want to kiss those women, or those men. I didn't want to kiss you, either. I wanted to reach for something inside you, suck your essence out through your mouth, like a parasite. That was all. We never talked about it. After all, what happened that last week on the island overshadowed all the alcohol, weed, and kisses that came before. But not yet, wait. Let me write a bit more about those careless days leading up to *it*.

The morning at the beach café, I remembered it only later when I started looking for some point in your chaotic story. We were drinking iced coffee and eating hard cinnamon cookies. The newspaper said that a maniac stabbed his wife and two kids to death in the same night. You read the news out loud, stopping after each paragraph to see my reaction. But I was busy checking out the young men who played beach volleyball in shorts so tiny that, from time to time, they revealed more than planned.

'What would you do if you read in the papers that I died?' you asked and slurped the last drops of your iced coffee so loudly that a woman next to us turned and looked at you with disgust.

'You gotta slurp that coffee like that?' I asked with a laugh so that you, naturally, repeated the slurping as loud as you possibly could. Once there was not a drop left in the glass, you licked your face and said, 'Seriously now. What would you do if I died?'

'Jesus, what . . . I'd be sad.'

'Sad? Just sad?'

'And bewildered . . . And hysterical . . . I don't know what you want me to say. I don't wanna think about that.'

'Problem is you never had anyone die,' you said. 'You're not ready.'

'My grandpa died.'

'That doesn't count. He was a hundred years old and you barely spoke.'

'What are you saying?'

'You're not ready. You're gonna go berserk when someone you know dies.'

Is that why you did it, a couple of days before we went back home? Was that the point? Just a few more days, Lejla, and everything would have been fine. The story wouldn't have broken in two. But it's done now, I have nothing left to write to put off the moment.

We swam far out, trying to dive with our eyes open. We jumped off the rocks and propelled ourselves deep down. You twisted in the water trying a somersault without success. I saw you climb the steep rock again, getting ready for another jump. I closed my eyes and dived deep, hearing your plunge a few feet away. I wanted to touch the bottom and get back. I didn't make it, fear got to me first and I changed my mind halfway down, it was too deep. Then I sprang out and saw your motionless body. You became *a body*. You were floating in the water like a leaf. The sun hit your unprotected back. Your face turned to the bottom of the sea, a lost look. Arms wide open as if someone pointed a gun at you under the water.

'Lejla?'

Nothing. No reaction.

'Stop that,' I said and pushed you. Your lifeless body just

moved away like a piece of wood. Black hair waved in the water like seaweed. You were dead in that moment; I saw your corpse.

You had drowned. I grabbed your shoulders and turned you face up. There was nothing human left in your face, no life, just a carcass. I started crying, screaming your name, and slapping you hard across the face. Some swimmers stopped moving in the distance, looking at us. The sun was unbearable. I kept hitting you until I realized you were holding my wrists and laughing.

'Sara! Hey, Sara! I was just screwing around!'

I was still shaking. You had already died in my memory, it had happened, even if you looked me right in the eye now, my wrists still in your strong grip, your cheeks alive and red from my slapping. Your legs were working fast in the water – keeping us afloat.

'What the fuck?!' I screamed and jerked my hands away from yours.

'Sara, calm down . . .'

'What is wrong with you?! Are you crazy?!'

I wanted to murder you, right there and then. To punish you for dying before my eyes.

'Sara, I'm alive,' you said and laughed. 'Here, touch me.'

You were having fun. It was so much fun to test people to death.

'You're deranged! You know that? You're sick!'

'Sara, you're overreacting.'

I burst into tears, couldn't hold it. My own fear scared me. Suddenly I realized it had all been a joke, the sea and your hair were nothing but props used to prove my naivete and how unprepared I was. I hated my own weakness, the fact you had seen me cry so many times.

That's when I said it. I don't know why. Perhaps to justify my stupid whimpering, give it some weight. It got out on its own.

'I got scared, Lejla . . . First Armin, now you.'

I regretted it instantly. Your face changed as if someone had suddenly turned the lights off inside you. A complete lack of sympathy. It scared me more than your fake death. I had touched the beast.

'What do you mean, *first Armin?*' you asked slowly. I was quiet, hiding behind my tears. *If your dad hears something.* I remembered the poster with Armin's face. *Daddy's doing what he can.*

You slapped me hard across the face. The hit surprised me, as if it didn't happen on purpose.

'Stop whining and answer me. What do you mean, *first Armin?*'

I started sobbing wildly, swallowing seawater. Entirely unmoved, you slapped my face again. My mouth was full of salt, the sun scorched my head. My legs were getting tired. I wanted to hold on to something, I couldn't keep afloat much longer. I reached for your shoulders instinctively. You pushed me away with contempt, as if I were a gelatinous lump of seaweed, and swam back to the shore.]

ten

Silence entered the car again, like an awkward hitchhiker of suspicious origin, as we stormed towards Zagreb. I was expecting something special to happen at the border: trouble with documents, trouble with the car, half a kilo of cocaine under the seat, or something similar. But in the end, it was so easy. At first, Bosnia tried to keep us in the cornfield, braiding Lejla's white hair along a dead stalk, swallowing us under its barren growth. But then it simply spat us across the border, just like that.

It was different this time; different from when I had first left. Back then I was alone, with two big suitcases and two pieces of paper which I kept in my coat as if my life had depended on them: one had my plane ticket printed on it, the other said I had been accepted to an MA program in literature by the worst of the eight Irish colleges I had applied to. I held those two papers as something more precious than a passport. I needed them to get rid of that other Sara who walked out of Lejla's room; Sara whose nails were still full of dirt from when she buried Rabbit.

We left that dark country together this time, side by side,

without any paperwork to comfort us. Now that I had taken Lejla out of it and knew that Armin was somewhere else, Bosnia had lost its entire purpose. Like someone had taken its two batteries out.

As our documents were being checked, I glimpsed a photo of a serious, white-haired woman in Lejla's passport. I could read *Lela Barun* under the police officer's fat finger. We went on without drama. I didn't want to look in the rearview mirror and see *my country* perish. I didn't want to see it crumpled in the tiny glass, hemmed in by the plastic frame that still had Lela Barun's wedding band tied to it. I wanted to remember it big and green, watery and alive, spread between the fingers. I wanted to remember it the way it never was, at least not to us.

That was the last time I saw Bosnia.

It was getting dark. Really, logically, expectedly dark, with heavenly bodies changing their positions. There was still a bit of sunlight hesitating at the edge of a wide valley. I could see falcons, tired and scrawny, yet still proud, still lethal to pigeons, rabbits, and small rodents. I could see cars full of families expecting seven days at the seaside to give them meaning – them, their beach beds, their tanning creams and stale marriages. It was a relief to be out of the thick, organic blackness. And yet, the relief was the kind a horror-movie heroine might feel when she thinks she's safe, though the viewer knows better. The viewer is always the first to see the killer.

That darkness I could almost touch in Banja Luka, taste its fibers on my tongue – once it enters your bloodstream and spreads to your lungs, liver, brain, you can never be clean again. Now and again it might excrete a coating on the surface of your skin, making it harder and colder, numbing it little by little, until everyday pleasures become entirely trivial, and that simple happiness you were counting on keeps slipping from your rough hands.

Lejla tried to start a conversation several times, but I would just nod, shrug, or say 'aha'. The math teacher was still before my eyes, his presence upsetting me more than the fact she had nearly killed us. I tried to remember his hands writing numbers on the blackboard, opening a textbook, and scribbling notes. Then I would transpose those hands onto Lejla's body, which had only just started blooming with adolescent heat, hesitant between the child and the woman. It made me sick. Not because I was jealous or even because he was so much older, but because one piece of the story had come to me second hand. I needed the other Lejla, with black hair and a whole hymen, the Lejla whom irony had not yet bitten, to tell me that chapter.

I didn't feel like walking around Zagreb. While I looked for a place to park, Lejla went to buy some food. She came back with two cold sandwiches, a jumbo pack of Honey Hearts, three Snickers bars, and two liters of Coca-Cola.

I bought us an impossibly hot night on the top floor of a small hostel without air-conditioning. Cathedral bells and music from coffee shops entered our claustrophobic, oven-like room. We shared the bathroom with the other guests on the floor. Lejla went to take a shower and, waiting for her turn in front of the locked toilet door, started talking to a guy next

door. I heard him sing something and she laughed her cheap
Lela Berić laugh.

I couldn't help it – I had to open the door just enough to be
able to hear them. Anything would do, a minimal cutout that
would help me assemble this new Lejla and realize what she
had become in the twelve years we hadn't seen each other.

'That's not how it goes,' I heard her giggle. 'It's *With Marshal Tito, the hero son . . .* and then something, I don't know . . .
we won't sit in hell?'

'*With Marshal Tito, the fat son, we won't fit in hell?'* her
interlocutor offered. She laughed as if this was the funniest
thing she had ever heard. I got closer to the door and peeked
through. She was leaning against the wall, playing with a
strand of her hair. She had mastered completely all the rules
of that empty cliché. Like one of those complicated quadrilles
I could never understand, which came naturally to her. Two,
three moves and the guy was bought.

She continued, the crooked smile on, 'I can't remember
the lyrics . . . *and we lift . . .* What do we lift?'

'*We lift the skirts . . .*'

'Ha, it's not skirts, you're so bad . . .' she said and hit his
chest with her towel.

'*We lift our feet to wet the street . . .*' the moron continued.

'*And squeeze . . .*' Lejla said, to which they both giggled.
'What do we squeeze?' she asked, giving him a dumb, broad
look of a naïve little girl.

'We squeeze a lot of things . . .' he answered and touched
her nose.

He must have been ten years younger than her, but it
obviously didn't matter. Lejla could melt and remodel herself

depending on the mold she was given. She had an innate sensor for whatever it was they wanted and was capable of turning into the exact thing they longed for, the thing they believed would complete them and interpret them correctly, give them a meaning, or at least fulfill a cheap dream in two frames of a porno. She could shrink down to only a handful of herself.

Even from a distance, I could see he had an erection. A dark-haired, plump girl walked out of the toilet finally and smiled with a shaky 'Sorry I took so long.' It soon turned out this was *his* girlfriend – he hung his soft arm around her and took her back into the room next to ours. Lejla winked at him before entering the bathroom.

Loud, overworked sighs came out of their room that night, the kind of sounds emitted by those women who think it's their fault if the sex is bad and the addition of secretly learned onomatopoeia would help them correct the injustice.

'Poor girl . . . Now she has to fuck that moron because you turned him on,' I said in the dark. I could tell she wasn't asleep; she kept fidgeting because of the heat.

'Wow . . . Sara has spoken! I thought you'd ignore me till Vienna.'

'Seriously. Do you have to flirt with every idiot you come across?'

'And do *you* have to patronize everyone who didn't study literature and didn't write a book and can't quote Crnjanski?'

'That's *so* not true.'

In the room next to us, the lover boy shouted, 'Do you like it?! Do you like it?!' which made both Lejla and me laugh out loud.

'He's putting on a show for you,' I said, 'he knows you can hear him.'

'Let them be . . . Let them love.'

'What if they make a kid today? Because he had a boner? That's on your conscience.'

'I didn't give him a boner. Tito did.'

'You're using our cultural and historical heritage to turn men on.'

'It's normally used for that purpose.'

The guy started yelling again, 'You want more?! You want more?!' We never heard the answer.

'Perhaps I have done a good deed. Maybe they make a smart little girl tonight,' Lejla said. 'A writer like yourself.'

'You have Dino. You can make little writers with him.'

That was the first time I'd mentioned him since we had left Mostar. The lover boy finally came on the other side of the wall. Lejla was silent. I felt we were something again, or at least a part of something which had existed before the island, now in the darkness of a Zagreb hostel which quite accidentally fell across our path and which we would forget soon after. I wanted to hear her talk, it didn't matter what about, and imagine different hair and eyes for her, black as they once had been.

'Why didn't you tell me about the math teacher?' I asked.

She was quiet for a while and then answered, 'I don't know. I guess I didn't want you to hate him.'

'What does it matter whether I hate him or not? I told you everything.'

'I don't know . . . No idea. I'm stupid,' she said. And then suddenly, out of nowhere, asked, 'Do you have a husband?'

'I don't have a husband. I have Michael. And an avocado tree.'

'What are Michael and the avocado like?'

'Michael is . . . big. A redhead. Does programming. And the avocado tree makes zero sense. Honestly, I don't understand how it's still alive.'

'You never liked houseplants.'

'I never did. Still don't,' I said and yawned.

After a while I thought she had fallen asleep. The hostel sailed into an ominous silence. We could only hear the cathedral. I realized that, if everything went as planned, I would see Armin tomorrow. I was afraid to say his name in front of her, as if I didn't have the right to it. Somewhere within me I still kept the shame of a twelve-year-old girl whose hair was untied by an older boy. I would give it away if I mentioned him to her. I tried to come up with something I would put to him, ask him, but everything seemed banal. Would we have coffee somewhere? Would he come with his wife and kids? How would I fit the blurred image of a sixteen-year-old god into an ordinary man who orders coffee and wipes his kid's nose? For a moment I wished our trip would never end, that there would always be another hostel, in whichever city, whatever time, where a different Lejla and a different Sara would lie and talk about teachers, plants, anything really, moving slowly toward the boy under the cherry tree. Maybe I realized a sad truth in that second – I didn't need Michael. I was fine, there on the bed in the stuffy room. *You never liked houseplants.* I never had to explain anything to her, she had the right magnifying glass for my inner turmoil. My blood was full of little dark specks that spread all over my body. Now I had to get used to them, accept them as something essentially mine, something that neither Michael nor all the other Michaels in the world will ever have the right sensors for. They might be intrigued at first, but will eventually just grow tired. Now and then they will sniff an illogical sadness on the edges of my being, a darkness shed by my skin, but won't know how to interpret it, regardless of all the well-meaning attempts. They will be angry because they are not *the one* who will fix me. They will read me from left to right, using a bunch of dictionaries, turning me into a hardcover book, and then Lejla will show up, tear out the pages, and make little birds out of them. Because she is the only one who knows you can't interpret darkness, it has no meaning, no theme. She is the only person who can free me from the cover boards.

'You know something . . .' Her voice suddenly came from the other side of the room.

'What?'

'About kids.'

'What about kids?' I asked.

'I can't, you know? There's something wrong down there . . . with the plumbing.'

I turned towards her, though I couldn't see her in the dark.

'You're a hundred percent sure?'

'A hundred thousand.'

'And you'd like to? Have kids, I mean.'

'I don't really know,' she said, 'I'd like to have a choice. Perhaps. I don't know.'

'Fuck . . . I'm sorry,' I whispered in a stupid voice. I didn't know what to say. Words came off wasted, ineffective again. Lejla did that to them – she could strip the fancy clothes off their frail bodies. We were quiet again and then, after some time, I could hear her deep, steady breathing. As always, she fell asleep before me.

I thought that this was it: two women in a little room without air-conditioning, with warm Coca-Cola on the table and the sound of the cathedral breaking through the squeaky window now and then – that was all. Someday, when we die, there will be no one to continue us. But the thought wasn't sad, at least not to me. That night I found comfort in it: two women who cut Bosnia in half and escaped the crime scene and who, one day, would simply stop. There would be no uncontrolled line of descendants meandering after us, we won't give this world any artists, whores, writers, any heroes or villains. We won't leave our names to some children who would call themselves *ours*, children who would grow old in a different time, and turn into people we would never meet. No one would ever be *us*. We were the only ones.

['This is you,' the teacher said smiling and pointed at the corkboard full of paper people. Our first day of school. The last memory, because it's the first. It's getting smaller, like a train dispatcher. I can hardly remember anything, so I'll have to invent half of it. But it doesn't matter; you'll remember the important bits. First I have to imagine fake scaffolding around weak memories, in order to preserve them. Ignore my empty storytelling. Remember the paper people. First day of school – they told us to design paper dolls that represented us. Mom bought several kinds of glittery paper, colored markers, stickers, and various stamps. We sat at the dining table that whole night trying to make *me.* The rule was clear – each child had to prepare their own figure *on their own*. This frustrated her. I colored over the lines, I cut off half of the foot, and the paper on the hair was way too dark.

'Again,' she said. 'Take this one . . . And careful with the scissors, don't ruin it all again.'

I cut out little people with skirts attached to their bodies and painted them *girl colors*. I rubbed glitter into their shaky limbs. I would look at Mom's face to see if I'd succeeded. She would recognize me in all that paper, she knows how to make me – she had done it once before. I wanted long green hair, all the way down to my feet, a dress made of leaves, and yellow eyes. But Mom said that's not good, did I want other kids to mock me? She took the scissors and cut out my paper doll, although she knew it was against the rules. But she's the mom, she knows best. I'm clumsy with scissors.

'Here,' she said and handed me a little girl made of pink paper. Her hair was prettier than mine, straight, with a little star in it. She was holding a flower, though I had broken our weeping fig the previous week. Mom had said that people who can't take care of plants couldn't take care of people either. But the little paper *me* knew how to take care of plants. The flower in her hand was the size of her head. She wore a pink dress I never had, and smiled with her red lips. Mom never let me use her makeup.

There's a queue in front of the school. Our mothers and us. Soon we will be summoned, let go of their hands and enter the building together, yet completely alone. Each one on our own, suddenly part of a group, part of something bigger than the family table.

Your mother is wearing a broad red dress and cork sandals. I didn't know people could be so beautiful. The way she touches her watch to check the time, the way she strokes your hair which is as black as her own, the way she laughs at something you said – you! So little, like me, you managed to make her laugh. I can't see you, your back is turned to me; you don't exist yet. At the same time, two equally strong emotions strike me: a desire to have *that* woman for my mother, with slim legs and a straight spine, a big white smile on her face, but also a feeling of guilt for wanting to replace the woman standing next to me. Later on you will insist that your mother never owned a red dress, that I must have mixed her up with someone else, but I held on to my memory like a lottery ticket.

I'm going to tell this one, like everything else. The school, a murky day, a sense of guilt squeezed between my palm and Mom's. They start shouting our names and chaos begins. A boy starts screaming, holding on to his mother's coat with both hands. Other kids look at him as if he were an orchestra conductor and, taking their cue, start crying in the same rhythm – some squeal, others sob quietly, and bewildered mothers glance at each other in shame, pretending to be astonished. *This never happens to mine; this is all your fault.* That's when I see you. You start to exist. The real *you*, without a name.

You are the only kid who's not crying. I'm on the verge; my chin is already shaking, not because I'm afraid to let go of my mom and enter the school, but because crying seems to be the first collective action of our group. Something to be done. But I can't cry while you're looking at me.

As if you know, you keep on staring. A whole choir of spoiled brats scream around us. Teachers come to fetch them; they hold them like furniture and take them clumsily into the building. Mom is proud of me – all the other women have seen that her daughter doesn't cry – the police chief's daughter. I'm holding a pink paper *Sara* in my hand. I enter the school full of myself, as if I have liberated the city from barbarians, all the while knowing the heroic title is undeserved – they don't know that I'm a crybaby really. I hadn't even met you yet, and you managed to turn me into a different person, a better version of me. Now I would have to pretend I was a girl who didn't cry as long as you and that school existed.

The mothers stay outside, tired smiles on them, sad and excited at the same time, like a bunch of groupies after an emotional concert. All their meaning is inside the building, their common denominator. They are out of kids and now have to make small talk without protection. We are inside, each one with our own paper doll, eager to accept a new authority and all the rules that come with it. It's what we know.

Am I remembering it right? I have to twist it and invent, there is not enough language yet to weave strong memories, only sensations are left: the steady fissures on the little table, smoothed by the palms of hundreds of children who came before us, the bitter breath of kids who never brush their teeth, chalk squealing on the blackboard, light circling across pictures in our textbooks, the sweet taste of sticky bread rolls during lunch break. You will tell me I invented the whole thing, nothing was the way I remember it, which school did I go to? But my inventions are closer and clearer to me than mere school documents, faded class photos and your surgically precise memory.

Yet some images remain, some are simple and ordinary, precisely because I didn't invent them. Those two boys who sat between you and me, talking about their *peepees*. You and I look at each other, we know something is wrong, though we're not exactly sure what. The teacher is far away, looking at the blackboard. That thing the boys are discussing – we don't

have that, it's the *other* thing, theirs only. All the shame and
fear of our world lie in that difference. We get the answer too
soon, wrinkled little answers to a question we didn't know we
carried. The two boys unbuttoned their trousers and showed
their *peepees* to each other as if comparing their pencil cases. I
look at you – you tilt your head and observe their tiny penises
uncertain what they were used for, with a kind of sympathy
for the unpractical deformation on their bodies. That's when
I see them too, having seen them in your eyes first – the two
crippled mushrooms in the middle of those boys.

I can't remember how or when the frightful spectacle
ended. We sat with each other from that day on, drawn
together not only because we were afraid of those bodies, but
also for the sense of complicity in our difference. A confusing
mix of disgust and awe brought us together. We were *you and I*.

I can't remember the first time you told me your name,
either. Sometimes it seems like it has always been there, like I
had known it from the first moment – though I realize that's
impossible. What I do remember is the paper doll you brought
to school, your *Lejla*. She was white, cut out from thick art
paper. There were no eyes, no lips, no nose. You didn't cut
her body so it spread into a skirt; you added no details. The
teacher gathered our little paper people and started fixing
them to the corkboard next to the map of the world. She
pierced our heads with little pins. Our arms and legs twisted,
they would flutter each time someone opened the classroom
door.

When she saw your paper doll, she asked why you hadn't
colored it. I can't remember a single detail from the classroom, I can't remember the children's faces and textbooks,

but I know what you replied. Your language has always had that effect on me – like the mechanical needle recording music on vinyl.

'It's the skin,' you said. Some kids laughed meanly, hiding their envy. Your paper doll was different from everyone else's. The teacher would remember you first.

'What about the clothes?' she asked.

'Well, it's not like I wear the same clothes every day.'

That's all I remember. She didn't want to insist; your father had died recently so she would be kind for forty days, as is the custom. And my colorful paper doll, full of glitter, with a flower in her hand, was suddenly stupid and exaggerated. I felt ashamed before your simple truth. That was the first time I thought someone might know more than my mother. It was embarrassing to think that way, I wanted to protect her – so pitiful, with a bag full of bright papers and colored stickers – protect her from your brutal exactness. Perhaps I broke in two then: the one who accepts your truth, aware of her lie on the corkboard, and the other one, who would go home after school and fulfill Mom's dreams of the little girl in pink. And perhaps it went further than that: perhaps that's when I imagined a whole me for the rest of the world, something I would never dare show you, afraid you would see through my pretense. That's why it was so easy to leave, change the language, pronounce my own name differently, pretend that somewhere far away, in the dark heart of Europe, you didn't exist.

We didn't share much during that first year of friendship. You told me you didn't have a dad, I told you I didn't have a brother. To my childish brain death and nonexistence were the same thing – a mere absence. But that didn't matter because you accepted me, as if I had been assigned to you. As if this story had existed before us. After we had witnessed those unbuttoned boys, we became inseparable. We hadn't done anything wrong, but we knew some kind of shame was there, something that could be used against us. There was no need to look for another reason to stick together. You told me you had an older brother. You invited me to your seventh birthday. The neat bureaucracy of first friendships. And what were we then, what did *Lejla and I* come down to? A bit of flesh and humanity.

I can't beautify those days, I can't give them some special, big meaning. You would despise me for it. Besides, I don't know how to write those two kids: you keep shrinking and growing in my memory, like illusive land to desperate sailors. I add an older you into those few recollections I have, the one groped by our math teacher, the one who lost her virginity next to me, by the river. That older, disappointed Lejla is massacring my naïve memories of careless *childhood friendship*. I wanted to go back and explain everything, but it seems I just got further away and managed nothing. In fact, I only got lost.

I don't know, Lejla. And I have to know, right? Would you like that? An omniscient narrator? Perhaps you were right the whole time, perhaps there are no points, no hidden patterns under the surface of life. I wanted to walk backwards, to connect the dots, one, two, three, like those drawings by numbers you so loved as a kid. But you never wanted that, did you?

My explanations, the violence of my meaning. I was

supposed to just spread out some images. I was supposed to put you in a story, you – a simple Mostar waitress, entirely ordinary, a woman who would leave nothing behind, except perhaps the bones of a rabbit and a tampon tossed into the night. Only fools like me can put you in a book. But, you see, all stories have one inevitable property – sooner or later they must end. And, as you well know, there's nothing after our ending. Remember that day on the island when you told me I wasn't prepared for death? *You* are the one who's not prepared. And each new word brings us closer to the end.

I know that fear of yours. I recognized it at the very beginning, though I never said so. The day we walked into the classroom and your paper doll was missing from the corkboard. All the colorful cardboard and glitter and stickers, and your simple white *Lejla* nowhere to be seen. You thought I hadn't noticed, right? You pretended not to care, that it didn't matter. Where the little paper *you* once hung, a piece of unadorned cork stood empty. The void sneaked out of the board and found its way into your chest. I saw the whole thing, nothing was lost on me: the way you tried hard not to show your fear, the anguish of someone who had just witnessed their own disappearance. A jealous child must have snatched your paper doll. They didn't even try to get the pin out first, they probably ripped your forehead, crumpled you, and tossed you in the bin, together with hard breadcrumbs and dried apple peel. Maybe because of the first A you got in math. Maybe because your simplicity reminded them of their excessiveness. Does it matter, anyway? Somebody stole you while you weren't looking.]

eleven

I must have been driving through Slovenia for half an hour when I realized that Bosnia had stayed far behind us a country ago. Perhaps because I could still feel her between us, as if we had driven through cinders. *We're always in Bosnia.* Now we were spreading her all over Europe. Our country with its irreconcilable borders was, in fact, borderless. We had fought for nothing, killed each other over nothing. We were never *inside* that country – she is the one inside *us* like a phantom itch. Our skin bleeds from futile scratching.

Once Michael and I watched a sci-fi series in which a boy is kidnapped by alien beasts and taken to their world of darkness and despair. In the end he's saved and goes back home to his desperate mother. However, in the last episode, when the boy goes to the bathroom to wash his hands, he feels sick all of a sudden and starts throwing up into the washbasin, vomiting those same parasites that had taken him. There's no more cleanness for him. As I watched the scared boy on Michael's big TV screen, I realized that I knew the feeling. But I didn't say anything. Michael wouldn't have understood anyway.

*

We stopped to get gas and go to the toilet. When I came back to the car, a Roma boy was cleaning our windshield. 'You don't have to do that.' I tried to stop him, but it didn't work. He wiped the glass in moves befitting a master painter. I realized nothing would stop him, so I sat in the car waiting for Lejla. She soon showed up with a jumbo pack of chips and a chocolate bar.

'You're exploiting child workers,' she said when she got in the car.

'I told him to stop, but he wouldn't listen.'

When he finished the windshield, he moved on to the windows, regardless of my protesting. I was uncomfortable. I wanted to be the mature, educated, socially aware person who doesn't support and enable capitalist tyranny. But the boy looked so happy that someone had finally let him do the job that I couldn't bring myself to hurt his feelings with my pompous, white *justice*. In the end I opened the window and put several euros in his rough hand. Before he left, he stopped in front of our car and gave a deep bow, a ceremonious look on his face.

'As if we were king and queen . . .'

'I'm the queen,' Lejla said.

'Lucky us,' I answered and turned the ignition. The immaculate spotlessness of the glass in front of me made me feel guilty.

When did Slovenia become Austria? I don't know. It seems like our itinerary spread out and twisted that May, following its own laws, far from exact cartography. As if we had pressed a glass board over someone else's map – their names,

countries, and borders were visible underneath, but a different surface existed for the two of us – slippery and uniform.
Somewhere on its edge we could see Armin and his black coat,
though he must have grown out of it by then. I was hoping
Lejla would mention him now that we had reached Austria,
but she kept devouring chips and singing primitive melodies
as if we were going on a high-school trip. I decided to interpret that as a defense mechanism. I had no right to mention
him first; she had to be the one to do it. Every time I wished
to say his name, I would feel the cold sea around my legs and
Lejla's slap burning across my cheek. So I talked about everything else: the weather, the food, people who went to our high
school and whose stories we didn't know. She told me that the
tennis racket was a present from Dino, which made me crack
up. Lejla, at least the one I had known, could perhaps solve a
chess problem or a math puzzle faster than anyone, but she
always sucked at sport. Once, the PE teacher kicked her out
of class because she interrupted a basketball game to read
the letters on the ball. Giving sporting equipment to such a
person could mean either utter ignorance or cruel mockery.

'You and tennis . . . Poor Dino,' I said.

'And I suppose you and avocado make a great couple?'

'Well, no. But seriously, Lejla. A tennis racket. Have you
ever used it?'

'I have. Dino was my coach. That's how we met.'

'Coach? Tennis coach? You took *tennis lessons?*'

'For about a month in total. I couldn't take it anymore.
All that running after the ball like a dog . . .' she said, looking
through the window at Austria's plastic skin. 'Poor guy still
thinks I'll come back.'

I wasn't sure whether she was talking about tennis or her marriage in general, but she interrupted my thought before I could ask.

'What's that?' She pointed her finger at some water barely visible in the flattened green.

'No idea. A lake, I guess . . .'

'Let's go there!'

'Come on . . . We're almost in Vienna.'

'But I wanna see the lake,' she said calmly, as if offering an irrefutable fact against which no argument of mine would work. Then I remembered how she had almost killed us in the cornfield and so I decided it would be easier to take a thirty-minute break for her to see some stupid water than risk a car accident all over again.

The lake was artificial, and so was the parking lot, and so was the grass, and so were the waitress's nails when she brought our coffee and kindly asked Lejla to get her feet off the chair. It seemed like someone had stretched foil across the surface of the water, as if an unexpected stone would rip the whole view like a photograph. Each grass stalk looked the same size, like a hair-removal salon had taken care of the lawn, not a gardener. And the green was so different from our green – it had the same uniform hue wherever I looked: at the trees, the hedges, the grass . . . It reminded me of that little Microsoft bucket you click on to fill up a shape with one even color. Birds sounded the same in their synchronized harmony, delivering as if on cue perfect thirds and fifths, so I thought we must have been listening to a CD instead of real beaks. I remember how I used to appreciate such things:

streets without litter, evenly cut hedges, clean benches, and the overall orderliness of *the world abroad*. I couldn't stand it now. Not because Bosnia and its carelessness were any better. I have never been one of those people who are proud of signs of their own failure as if these were proof that *us locals* are more heartwarming than *them foreigners*. But in that moment, with the disappointed Lejla looking at the perfect square lake and shouting, 'Oh, fuck me!' when she read the price of two coffees, Austria irritated me. I felt wrong compared to its immaculate grass – my edges were rough, my skin uneven, my thoughts colored over the lines. That's when I realized I didn't like *manufactured landscapes* – they made me feel like my humanity was a mistake, a deeply personal flaw. Suddenly I had a strong urge to piss in that lake.

I attributed this to Lejla's presence too – perhaps if she hadn't been sitting next to me, I would have played the role of a *civilized European*. In fact, I would have enjoyed it. But she always reminded me of something within me, something fundamental that could never fit within four perfect corners. She reminded me that disorder was the natural state of the world and that our lives, organized around the effort to bring order to that chaos, were nothing more than a reflection of our vast arrogance.

Lejla looked up at the sun and closed her eyes. I could see the roots of her hair, black like blindness against the Austrian light. As if a pinch of darkness had sneaked into it before we had left Banja Luka. I felt stupidly happy to have witnessed the real color of her hair, as if it meant I had won some argument we had been having since Mostar. The black roots meant I hadn't invented all of it – somewhere inside that woman there was the real Lejla who would break out to the surface sooner or later.

In front of us, two girls were spinning around on the grass and kept falling down in real, prepubescent laughter. The taller one had very white skin and her hair had such a light color that it looked like she would disappear if she got any closer to the sunlit part of the lawn. She was wearing short overalls and a white T-shirt which, compared to her hair, looked almost yellow. The other one had a thick red bun and, as she turned around with her arms spread and eyes closed, her green dress turned with her like a gentle propeller ready to launch her high up above the lake. Their mothers were sitting close to us, chit-chatting in German without taking their eyes off the lawn. From time to time, one of the girls would get dangerously close to the lake, entranced in her dance, until her earthly mother shouted something and broke the spell. The sentence would stretch between the mother and the daughter like a leash and pull the disobedient girl away from the water.

'I never told you to go fuck yourself,' Lejla said all of a sudden, her eyes still closed.

'What are you talking about?' I asked, looking at the two girls, envious of their natural carelessness and the fact they could fall on the grass without anyone thinking them crazy.

'When we last saw each other, when we buried Bunny.'

'You opened the door and told me to go fuck myself,' I said, 'I remember it quite well.'

She opened her eyes wide and sat up straight in her chair.

'It's amazing how much you enjoy inventing things . . .'

'I'm not inventing anything,' I said calmly. I remembered a police show I had seen once. During training, police officers were taught how to handle psychopaths. *You can't lose your temper at any point – it's a sign of weakness.*

'Sara, you're kidding, right?'

'Jesus, Lejla, what does it matter? It happened a hundred years ago. And I'm no longer mad about it.'

'Well would you look at that . . . *I'm no longer mad about it*. First she invents the whole damn scene and then she congratulates herself for not being mad about it.'

'I really don't feel like talking about this now.'

One of the girls, the paler one, had stopped spinning. Something had gotten her attention, something in the air. She was standing in the middle of the lawn staring right before her, while her red-haired friend still turned around with her eyes closed.

'Listen to me,' Lejla said, suddenly adamant, 'I asked you – *Where are you going?*'

'Lejla, it really doesn't matter . . .'

Something in the air, the pale-skinned girl saw something. Like an invisible butterfly. She followed its bewildered dance.

'And then you told *me*, quote, *I'm gonna go fuck myself.* And then I opened the door and you left. Curtains, end of story.'

'Lejla, that girl . . .'

'What girl?'

'The blonde one, in overalls,' I said and pointed at the lawn, 'something's not right.'

And that's when it started – one small elbow jerked up in a peculiar way, as if an invisible teacher pulled it hard. The blonde girl fell on the ground and went into violent spasms. The other girl covered her face with her hands and took a few steps away from her friend – who was no longer herself. The small body twisted wildly, as if uprooting itself from the ground beneath, moved by an unreachable neuro-logical error, reminding all the witnesses that we were nothing but a sad collection of fallible molecules.

The mothers ran towards the girls, their high heels left wounds on the grass. Everyone stood up and stared at the tiny being which continued convulsing uncontrollably: the waiters interrupted their itineraries as if trying to remem-ber whether this kind of situation could be considered part of the job; other guests exchanged worried glances, waiting for someone else's intelligent comment, someone had to know what needed to be done. But the mother was up to the task – that little woman with skinny arms who wore an ugly sparkly dress and a ridiculously tall hairstyle – she was the only expert in what was going on, the most scared of, and the most ready for, her daughter's spasms.

After a while the attack weakened and the girl just lay in the grass, as if relaxing after a long day spent playing. The ambulance arrived late – the worst was over. The mother was explaining something to the paramedics, who nodded in agreement. One by one, the waiters moved again and the audience went back to their chairs slowly, sharing worried glances, as was proper. The sound of synchronized birds was back, it seemed they had gone silent during the frightful scene. Lejla and I kept standing by our table, looking at the small group of people by the lake. I remembered our summer on the island and realized that perhaps she was right. I *was* unprepared. Not just for death, but for anything out of the ordinary. This kind of situation could only paralyze me, those terrifying scenes during which our real nature showed its true self. Compared to that mother, so efficient and without any drama, I felt entirely useless. In that moment of silent terror, it dawned on me that I would never save anyone, I would never run across some lawn to help someone, I would never find the important pill in time, I would never be that person in a restaurant who would perform the Heimlich maneuver on someone who is choking. I would just stand there in my silent paralysis and watch death spread around me.

'Poor kid,' Lejla said.

'Yeah, she could have really hurt herself,' I said, still dumbfounded, 'imagine if she had fallen in the lake.'

'Not her,' she answered. I looked at her in confusion. Her eyes were wet, which caught me completely off guard. I followed her gaze and realized that she was talking about the other child, the one in the green dress. The red-haired girl stood frozen some distance from the paramedics, the mothers, and her exhausted friend, and was sobbing inconsolably, her face in those tiny, freckled hands.

[My hands are tired, with occasional throbs of pain which no doctor in Dublin – at least no doctor I could afford – could explain. Sometimes it feels like I've been typing for a decade. Every now and then I have to stop and massage my hands – at times the pain is dull, spilling over the joints; other times it's sharp, right there in my fingertips. Then I have to stop with my hands in the air above the keyboard and wait for it to go away. Tense and twisted, they look more like a pair of ragged claws, their red skin coming off in dust. You would tell me to stop whining, some people have real problems. Therefore, I allow myself ten-second breaks only.

But it feels like I got it all wrong. The letters are here, I could scroll through the text and go backwards, change everything that happened, dress you in better clothes, put green contacts in your eyes, resurrect the dead Rabbit. But I can't. I want to get to the end, close the laptop, massage my hurting hands, and go outside. Besides, it's scary to change direction now. Going backwards would mean turning the car around and driving back to Bosnia. That would kill my story. Hence – let's go on. Damned hands like two spiders. Standing in one place, devouring dead meat. And I was supposed to write you a simple scene, polish a single memory. Somewhere where your hair isn't blonde and the seaweed doesn't stink on that island. A single happy day.

Is that what you wanted?

All right. I can't go back, but it doesn't matter. Just forget everything up to this point, OK? Let's start again:

'I'm going,' you said, 'to buy a white rabbit.'

A crack appeared somewhere in the gloom, letting through a weak, yet unmistakable ray of light. Our town was sleeping, unaware of the sunshine that revealed it. I didn't know that excitement then, where it came from. Now it seems to me that on that very morning after prom we felt the power of being stars of our own story. We were given the role of the hero, since everyone else was asleep. I say *hero* and not *heroine*, because the latter didn't exist back then; they were hidden like shameful secrets, pushed to the corners of bad books with their skirts up, or forgotten in unkempt graves, like poor Safikada. But that day, when a thin ray of light decided to spare our town for one morning, we took on the role of the protagonist. I could feel it – though I didn't know what it was – the power to do whatever we felt like. Everything existed for us and because of us: the treetops with birds exploding out of them, the decrepit walls of Kastel, the broken branches carried away in the fast river, the smells sneaking out of the waking bakeries, the desolate streets with mutilated sidewalks – they were ours.

You ran across the long bridge, a thin denim jacket fluttering wildly behind you, your black ponytail beating like a mad bird's wing, and I ran after you, slow, red in the face, still hurting between the legs, but happy nevertheless. It felt like we were the only two people in that town: the bridge was empty, *kafanas* were closed, venetian blinds pulled down.

Two deflowered brats with ten marks under the elastic band of your leggings, and a single sunny day. What else did we need?

Even when we got to the market where rosy-cheeked women lined up sad-looking tomatoes and bell peppers in wooden crates, and men put underwear and nylon stockings on the rickety stalls, it seemed like they were there for us, like extras in *our* story.

'Where do we find a rabbit?'

'I know a guy,' you answered, as if we were getting cocaine.

We bought Gummi Bears and a plastic yo-yo that had a face of a footballer on it. I felt my lost virginity as a newly acquired foreign language. Suddenly everyone around me – salespeople, hobos and beggars, bakers and florists – became *people who did it*. Did anything give me away? The way I walked perhaps, the way I laughed, the way I jerked the poor footballer's face from my hand towards the dirty ground and back again? Something within me wanted to reveal the secret, for people to look at me and see experience, as if I had defended a doctoral thesis and not spread my legs under some boy.

You seemed to be more excited about the rabbit than the first time you'd had sex. You had that aura of careless-ness that I would copy for young Dubliners so they would remember me. It seemed like you were always on a mission – get the condoms, buy the rabbit, take the rear seat in the bus – which made other people's motives look utterly lame. You approached these tasks with the seriousness of a market analyst, all the while making sure I knew you were bored, that it was just another job to be done. Four years later the rabbit would be dead, you would be blonde, and I would hold a shovel. But we don't know that then, rabbits don't die in that moment. We don't know that we have a year of friendship left, that there's an island waiting for us like a witch's house at the end of the forest.

At the dead end of the market, Mr. Kraljević is sitting on stacked beer crates, adjusting the beret on his bald spot. His perfectly ironed bird-patterned shirt is showing itself up in two dark circles at the armpits. He is surrounded by a bunch of cages, big and small, wooden, plastic, metallic, like a confused tyrant-god of a tiny animal kingdom. He is sitting with his hands on his knees, spreading his legs to make room for a huge belly. He's frowning, looking at the other sellers like an angry football referee. He reminds me of those people who are annoyed by everything, who always find the world an inch too small so that their awareness of themselves and their own presence is more than they can stand. And yet, he seems to be unbothered by the squealing around him – the rattling of the little wheels spinning under hysterical hamster legs; minute beaks singing for food, sex, or both; tiny teeth munching lettuce leaves. Only the turtles are silent. They remind me of my secret buried under the pine tree in our front yard.

'You're the girl that called about the bunny?' he asks and looks at you suspiciously, as if he was the one buying it.

'Yes. The white one.'

'And it's gotta be white? I got this spotty fella to die for.'

The way he said this made it clear to us that the *spotty fella* was the worst possible option. The *spotty fella* must have rabbit syphilis or a behavioral disorder.

'It has to be white,' you answer. Straight as a Trojan hero, you stand and look at the sweaty seller without blinking. Before your gaze, Mr. Kraljević is nothing but one of the many guinea pigs around him.

'Everyone wants a white one, what's the matter with you people. Come on, kiddo, check the spotty one, it's cute as hell.'

You turn around and start walking away. I'm confused. I look at him, then at you, and immediately run like a loyal page after an evil queen who has just insulted everyone.

'Yo, kiddo! Hey, *bona*!' shouts Mr. Kraljević, and you halt. 'What's this fuss for, where's the fire?'

'Mister Kraljević, I don't have the whole morning,' you say. Maybe because you called him a mister, or because several other sellers were now looking at us, he finally got to his feet and told us to wait. He turned his back to us and entered the backstage jungle behind two large hanging oilcloths. I looked at you in wonder – I wasn't expecting the whole thing would turn into such a drama. But you just closed your eyes like a spiritual guru and nodded slowly – everything was under control.

He emerged carrying a huge wooden crate full of rabbits.

'Is it OK for them to be all together like that . . . in a single crate?' I asked, which seemed to insult Mr. Kraljević.

'If ten people can live under the same roof, damn too can bunnies.'

Bunnies. Frightened little balls. The stench was unbearable. I imagined ten people squeezed together in one apartment, the stinking of their sardined bodies and dirty-faced children with forgotten diapers. I felt sick.

There were three black bunnies in the crate, several mixed breeds, and two whites. Mr. Kraljević took one out and handed it to you. You took it gently between your scrawny hands, as if holding a human heart. I could almost see fear in your eyes.

'So,' Mr. Kraljević began, 'the hay, gotta have lots of hay, always fresh water, start with green vegetables in about a month.'

'Is it male or female?' I asked.

'What does that matter?' you said.

'It's a girl!' Mr. Kraljević said proudly, as if he had just delivered a baby. 'The other one's a boy.'

'We'll call you . . .' you said to the scared little rabbit and then turned to me in wonder. 'Sara, what are we gonna call her?'

I had never named anything in my life. Mom baptized my turtles, too; they had fancy names from Mexican soap operas – Cassandra, Esmeralda, and Marisol. If I picked a bad name, I would reveal my stiff mediocrity to you. On the other hand, if I refused to name the bunny, I would admit I'm not up to the job. But then the locksmith's stall started jingling and drew our attention. A couple of apples rolled down the slope.

'What's going on?' you asked no one in particular.

I felt the ground tremble slightly. I was saved. My father used to say, 'Don't worry, honey. It's just Banja Luka trying to sneeze.'

'An earthquake,' I said quietly, to which Mr. Kraljević's smile froze in terror.

'Oh, God, not again,' he said in mortal dread.

Like an outer expression of his inner turmoil, the animals started squealing and jumping: thin birds fluttered their wings behind the rusty bars, guinea pigs got up on their rear legs wildly looking for answers, and the turtles conveniently retreated back into their shells. You and I were crouching, looking at each other calmly, as if our stare could overpower the tectonic plate. The rabbits had it best – since the crate was opened, they jumped out of its stinky hay and started running away in all directions. The unnamed *girl* disappeared from your hands, or did you drop her out of fear? I never asked you that.

Unlike the other rabbits who hid behind crates, ran down the hill, or disappeared behind the oilcloth curtains, the white *girl* made her way straight down the asphalt that separated the two lines of stalls. She was gone in a second, before we managed to name her. Mr. Kraljević ran after her, without thinking, his broken flip-flops clapping dangerously through the market. His fat belly jumped up and down as if it was trying to run away from its owner.

The earthquake soon weakened and the frightened sellers could relax again, at least those of them who were too young to remember 1969. They rearranged the fallen items, hung little bags with socks and underwear back on the protruding nails, caught up with the rolling apples, and exchanged bad jokes in order to get rid of the embarrassment of having showed fear.

A single rabbit remained in the crate – the white *boy*. You frowned at him, why didn't he run away like the others? He could have been free, instead of waiting here in an open crate for his fat tyrant. And then you looked at me. The look was quick, no words, but I got the message. Kraljević was still gone, running after his fugitives, though he could have been back any moment. There was no time to think – I took the little rabbit with both hands and put it in my wide cloth bag. I closed the zipper – he could breathe through the knitted rosette – and made it towards the exit. My own calm surprised me – I walked slowly, steadily, as if I had stolen a hundred animals before that. The rabbit was still; I could feel his warm body breathing against my thigh. I knew you were following me, but I didn't want to turn around. I was afraid I would see Mr. Kraljević running after us, all red-faced and angry, with his big belly like a mad avalanche of meat.

We were quiet until we passed through the large wooden door of Kastel and climbed one of its walls. We crouched at the lookout point, which made me think of a skillful Ottoman soldier who had once perhaps, from that same spot, observed Austrian infantry surround the castle. Two high-school gradu-ates with a hangover were there now, afraid not of the Royal Guard, but of an overweight pet-seller. You got up slowly and stood on your toes to see the market better. How big you looked to me then, stretched out and straight between the turrets, ready to defeat the whole Habsburg monarchy with one look.

I was ready to spend the whole day on top of Kastel, sitting on the grass with a little rabbit in my bag, leaning against the warm stone, while you kept watch for all the forces of the outside world. I proved something to you that day, at least I wanted to believe I had. I committed a crime for you, without a second's hesitation. What is more, it wasn't jewelry I had stolen, or a stupid T-shirt, or money from some careless idiot's pocket. No, I had stolen a *living thing*. Now you would know I was cool, that I could do anything and that, just like you, *I had no sense of boundaries.*

'Can you see him? Is he after us?' I asked.

'Nah . . .' you said. 'He's probably still running after the animals. Didn't even notice.'

'Poor guy,' I said, 'lost all of his rabbits.'

'Why *poor*? They're not *his* rabbits.'

'Whose rabbits are they then?'

'Nobody's,' you answered. 'Their own.'

'And you think they're gonna make it? Roaming the town on their own?'

'Maybe they'll leave town,' you said and smiled. 'They're fast.'

Clouds broke up the sky in bites. The town was waking up. Darkness was silently returning into its well-loved armchair. The bit of sun that had revealed itself for our criminal adventure had now retreated back through the crack, leaving us with dusk. I could see miniature people walking hastily down crooked streets. I could see venetian blinds opening up, like eyelids across gray buildings. I could see cars parking one by one on the lot where the Ferhadija Mosque once stood. 'A rocket,' you had told me a long time ago, second or third grade, while we were walking by that mosque. 'My dad once said that it was a rocket. But it's not, he was just kidding. It's called a minaret.' I thought of that while we were sitting on Kastel. I also remembered my thirteenth birthday, the one you couldn't come to. I had sat in my room with a couple of our classmates and laughed at school gossip while my happier than usual mom snapped photos with her little camera. Later on I threw those pictures away, afraid you would see them and learn what a good time I had had in your absence. A few days after that birthday the Ferhadija Mosque was destroyed. The rockets really flew up into the sky, leaving ugly parking lots behind them.

'Is he alive?' you asked me, sitting down on the dry grass.

I unzipped the bag and peeked into it. A furry white ball was still breathing inside.

'Totally,' I said. 'What are you gonna call him?' I asked quickly, afraid you would make me choose a name again.

'Nothing,' you said. 'He's better off without a name.']

twelve

Vienna is *swollen like a corpse*. Perhaps this story would be better if I could remember buildings, parks, and bridges. I could look them up, add street names, landmarks, sound well-informed. But in that moment Vienna was not a city – it was a monotonous maze. Armin was somewhere in it. Everything else: the glimmering clothes stores, clean cars parked next to cleaner houses, pompous statues with bird feces scrubbed off by men in uniforms – all that was of no importance. In fact, there was something fake about all this convenient beauty. As if someone had constructed the city overnight, scattered some people around, together with their lives and little churches, so that it would greet us enormous and brimming with history, and thus make it more difficult for us to get to Armin. I expected a logistical glitch at every corner, something to prove that the city wasn't real. If I entered the first shop and asked a simple question, everything would fall apart. I didn't trust that Vienna. As if it was that city that had poisoned those dogs and thrown Ozren Habdić's body in the cold river. As if it had sucked the light out of my own town. It was easier to think that way – to have a glorious culprit within arm's reach.

'Where . . .' I asked once we got to the center.

'Just find a parking spot. We'll find a hotel.'

'But aren't we gonna . . .'

'What?'

'I thought we were gonna . . .'

'Tomorrow,' she said. 'Tonight we eat and sleep. We deserve it.'

I felt a relief when she said that. I wasn't ready to see Armin yet. Not after the scene at the lake.

The Fröhlicher Jäger hotel was small and full of stuffed animals. Schlager music and French chansons filled the lobby. A photo of a fat, red-haired man hung behind the reception desk. He was holding a giant salmon on a hook. I suppose he was the owner and perhaps the person who had killed all those heads and horns that adorned the walls.

Lejla insisted on paying for the room, despite my protests. We got the key on a wooden keychain – a bear's head with the number 42 carved on the back. We climbed up to the little room. Everything in it was fake oak – the bed, the closet, the table, the mirror frame . . . Even the tiny TV set stood in a box of similar material. An oval picture in needlepoint hung above the bed – a lustful shepherdess with prominent breasts. She had a mistake in her left ear – someone had used the wrong thread.

'If there was a fire, all this shit would go up in flames in two seconds,' Lejla said, looking around.

'No, they varnish it with some sort of product . . . protection. It's the law.'

'So what? Like it doesn't burn just the same . . .'

'Well, it's just to protect it, so it's not just dry wood . . .'

She opened her bag, took out a red lighter, and lit it. A long flame danced in the darkness of our room.

'Should we check?'

'Lejla, that's not funny. Turn it off.'

She smiled and put the lighter back into her purse. She wasn't crazy yet. Crazy *enough*. Then she took her shoes off and threw herself on the big bed, which squeaked sadly.

'And what is that lighter for? You haven't started smoking, have you?'

'No. I just happen to have a lighter. It's one of those basic things.'

'Basic things?'

'Yes. For survival.'

I sat next to her on the bed and took her purse from the floor. Then I turned it inside out and spread its contents across the bedsheet. Lejla didn't mind. She lay on her belly to see what I was doing.

'Are these *basic things*, too?' I asked. 'Tissues, tampons, lipstick . . . A knife. For God's sake, what do you need a knife for?'

'To open something. Or peel it. Or kill it.'

'Four, five . . . Six boxes of condoms. Six. One isn't enough? Are you gonna fuck half of Vienna?'

She turned on her back and closed her eyes.

'You never know,' she said. 'In any case, I'm not dying of syphilis.'

'You can't die of syphilis nowadays.'

'You don't know that.'

She got up and walked to her suitcase. There was a heap of crumpled clothes and she pulled a black dress out of it. She pressed it to her body and checked herself in the mirror.

'A compass. You have *a compass*,' I said, checking the little metal gadget on the palm of my hand. The needle swayed like a drunken man's hand.

'Jesus, is this a trial? What's wrong with having a compass?'

'I'm not sure which era you're living in. Syphilis, compass . . . Now you only need one of those fin-de-siècle iron vibrators.'

'I don't need a vibrator,' she said from the mirror and her long fingers danced above her head. 'I've got these.'

'What's the dress for?' I asked.

'Dinner is included. With the room, I mean.'

'Do we really need to wear dresses to go down and have dinner? Have you seen this place?'

'OK, let's live in tracksuits and stop showering and grow hairs on our legs and go back into the cave and die and rot in our *naturalness* just because you don't like *this place*.'

An hour later I came down to the dining area in a gray cotton dress. It was the only one I had. Lejla was the star of the night in that sad place. Her dress was a size too big on purpose, so that it kept falling off one shoulder, dancing around her thin knees. It was meant to only insinuate the body beneath it and leave enough room for a lustful gaze to imagine that which wasn't clearly outlined. A long white braid, with a few strategically messy strands, glowed on the black synthetic material. But the restaurant was nearly empty – we went down too late. An old man was sitting at the corner table, finishing his soup with a shaking spoon. Besides him, there was only a quiet family. The mother had already finished eating; she was staring at her plate like someone who had just lost everything in a game of poker. The father violently broke off handfuls of bread and dipped them in his innocent soup. And the brown-eyed boy was quiet, moving his spoon around the melted ice cream in the glass bowl. Had they been fighting because of him? The boy-of-sponge. Someday something will press him and all the venom would leak out. It will burst over some other kid with melted ice cream on the table.

A plump hand wiped our table quickly. Neon light bounced off her purple nails while Lejla and I were busy commenting on the paintings on the walls. The waitress smiled and said, 'Well, I'll be damned . . . If you gals weren't my own folk, I wouldn't be servin' you. The kitchen closed a minute ago. But we'll find somethin', don't you worry now.'

We didn't manage to say anything, surprised to hear our own language in a Viennese hotel. The waitress then took small clipping scissors from the pocket on her apron and turned to Lejla.

'And you. You got a price tag hangin' on ya back. Can't go partyin' like that.'

She didn't wait for permission – the thin thread stretched between her purple nails and Lejla's dress, and she clipped the tag off in a blink. Then she crumpled it and put it in her apron pocket together with the scissors. It's like she felt responsible for the apparel of all *our countrywomen* in Vienna. We couldn't go around embarrassing her in the vast metropolis with our Bosnian price tags.

'Well, ain't that better?' she said and straightened the dress on Lejla's back. She sighed as if she had just tamed a beast. Then she took our orders, suddenly transformed into a professional waitress, and disappeared into the kitchen. I laughed.

'What just happened?' I asked Lejla.

'What happened is that I can no longer return this dress and get my money back.'

When *our countrywoman* appeared again, carrying a plastic tray with two big hamburgers and a bowl of fries, we kept straight faces. She said *enjoy* in German. Perhaps to show off her knowledge of the language, or maybe to punish us for not getting into a nostalgic conversation about *our country*.

We didn't talk about tomorrow and what awaited us there. A part of me wanted to go to bed early. I was planning what to wear, how to fix my hair, in order to remind Armin of the girl I used to be, but with a mature air that he would notice and appreciate. But another part of me hoped the night would be long. We would be *the three of us* tomorrow, like that day in their backyard. For now we were still *the two of us*, in simple dresses, in a small hotel in Vienna. Maybe that's why I said yes when she suggested moving to the hotel bar after dinner. I wanted us to last a little longer.

'You know,' she said after her second glass of wine, 'you are the only person in the whole wide world that still calls me Lejla.' A crystal ball hung from the ceiling, projecting colored crystals on her bare shoulder. Schlager music still played, entirely inappropriate for the dark, and the bar, and the alcohol.

'You're kidding?'

'I'm not kidding. I have been Lela for twenty years. Longer than that. Perhaps you haven't noticed.'

'There's no way your mom calls you Lela.'

'No, she calls me Leja. I couldn't pronounce my name when I was little. I would say *Leja. Leja thirsty. Leja pee.* So I stayed Leja to her.'

'Does it bother you that I call you Lejla?' I asked. I had never thought of it that way. There was pride in the way I addressed her, as if I were the only person holding a secret about her *nature*, her *essence*. But now I was sitting at the bar, drinking dark beer, realizing she was only eleven years old when they gave her a new name. I tried to picture an eleven-year-old. I couldn't. It dawned on me that the little *j* which I stubbornly added to her name was only there to give *me* the feeling that *I* was special, different. I saw my own vanity in that moment.

'You can call me whatever you like,' she said and raised her glass.

'I can't call you *Lela*, it's weird.'

'While you decide, both Lela and Lejla are gonna go pee.'

She went to the toilet on the other side of the bar, drawing interested looks from the business people and sad-looking couples from the surrounding tables. The toilet was busy, so she just leaned on the wall next to it and waved to me.

The opening notes of a chanson came from the big speaker above the fridge. I knew the melody; I always like that song. *The last time I was kissing you, cherries bloomed all around.*

How did they get that album in Vienna? But then the familiar song sprained my ears painfully – different words reached
me, in a foreign language, revealing the real nature of my
memory. Up till then, I had been certain that the song was
ours. My ignorance embarrassed me and I looked around as
if someone in the bar could have guessed my thoughts. Of
course it wasn't ours. As the song went on, it was more and
more obvious that it had never been ours. *But life is a different
thing, and the flame will die out soon.* No. French was perfect
for it. It was as if a woman, ten times more attractive than
me, had put my favorite dress on, revealing my flaws. Popular
French chansons used to be translated into our language and
recorded in different versions. I knew that. How could I be so
stupid?

I looked at Lejla, who was still waiting by the toilet. She
was listening to the song as well but, unlike me, she didn't
mind the French lyrics at all. She never really cared for words
anyway. Her head was tilted and she looked at nothing in
particular, with a barely visible smile on her face, as if she
had just found a long-lost toy. *Labranshe dan sareesyou do sone
zhardan caresseh* came loud from the speaker. She was somewhere else. Not in Vienna, not standing by the toilet door.
One part of the story lay between her and the song, a part
unreachable to me. She was no longer Lejla, either, but some
random girl remembering a fond memory. I longed to enter
her head and witness each frame. And more than that – I
longed to *experience* the music the way she did, to *become*
Lejla. Like back in those days I used to write her essays with
my pencil.

Perhaps it was just the alcohol, I don't know. I saw my

hands on the bar and wished to see her fingers instead of mine. I wanted my legs to stretch far out to the length of hers, my hair to grow long and turn white, I wanted to have her breasts and her ribs underneath and then – that way – hear the song. I reached for Lejla's glass and took a sip of wine. The acidity bit my throat. I was the fake one. The inadequate one. Armin would see that. The Venus from his backyard grew up into a mediocre little Miss May from a cheap gas-station calendar.

Meanwhile Lejla had gone into the toilet and closed the door behind her, unaware of my pathetic ruminations. How easy it was to be her, I thought, so careless and simple. Some people just *are*, without the drama. Lejla, or Lela, or Esmeralda. It didn't matter. And me? An average piece of rock imagining it was a volcano. I could still taste the bitterness of her drink. I never liked wine, it was about time I admitted it. I was sitting in the night bar of some Viennese hotel, looking at my hands. They were the most ordinary hands I had ever seen. I was looking at them for the first time in my life. *Zhecrou moureer damoor poorellah*, the French guy shouted on.

When she came out of the toilet, a tall guy in an expensive suit cut into her path. He had one of those messy hairstyles that cost half my salary. I couldn't hear them. I tried washing the bitter taste of wine out with some beer. The guy had his hands in his pockets and was saying something to her. Her shoulders shook in laughter. I wanted to disappear. Leja. Lejla. Lela. Which one was right for him? The chanson played on, putting me to shame with its fluid French.

Lejla tapped the tanned gentleman on the shoulder and came back to the bar.

'He wants to take a walk,' she said.

'Who wants to take a walk?'

'Franz Josef.'

'Franz Josef wants to take a walk. Who the fuck is Franz Josef?'

She nodded in the direction of his table and he put his glass up to us. A tiny crumpled beach umbrella peeked out of it.

'You're kidding me.'

'What's the big deal? I'm gonna go take a walk with Franz Josef. You should get some sleep, you've been driving for three days.'

'Lejla, you can't just leave with a stranger like that. You don't know who he is. Perhaps he has a basement full of enslaved women somewhere. Has it crossed your mind?'

'Sara,' she said seriously, 'go to bed.'

I wanted to add something, but she had already taken her purse and joined Franz, who was waiting by the exit.

'Ton't worry! I'll brink her back!' the clown yelled at me in terrible English, as if I had lent him a notebook.

I finished both the wine and the beer. I wanted to pay, but the bartender told me that *my friend's friend had taken care of it.* I felt like throwing up and left him a ridiculously large tip as if to let him know I was officially renouncing the good deed of Franz Fucking Josef. I took my purse and climbed up to room 42. I got in, took my shoes off, and lay on the large bed. The pillow was perfectly cold under my slight intoxication. 'Ich bin Lela,' I whispered into the empty space. 'Ich bin

Leja. Ich bin Lili.' I turned on my side and pulled my knees to my chest. There were wine stains on my dress. As if I had murdered someone. 'Ich bin Lulu. Ich bin Lala.' The little compass still lay next to me on the clean bedsheet. 'Ich bin Lo.' Its needle was trying to run away from my body as if I were toxic. It shook in fear towards the cold north.

The morning sun bounced off the fake oak unobtrusively, like a stranger apologizing for entering our room by accident. I woke up and saw a heap of white hair next to me. She came back. Quietly, I got out of bed and headed for the bathroom. On the little table next to the mirror I saw her Motorola, a lipstick, and three hundred euros.

'It would have been five if you'd joined us,' she mumbled behind me and yawned deeply. I turned to look at her. She moved to the middle of the bed, her arms and legs spread wide. Like that day by the river. *Gaudeamus igitur.* Smudges of mascara and blush transformed her pretty face into a sad clown.

'I don't understand. What would have been five?'

'Oh, Sara, you should have seen him . . . Kneeling before me. Wanted me to yell at him and hit him. *Bad boy. Fery bad boy.* Then he licked me for half an hour.'

She turned on her belly and stretched her arm towards the chewing gum on the bedside table. I kept looking at the money as if it were a camouflaged insect waiting to jump and inject me with its venom if I touched it. Had Franz thought he'd slept with a professional and mistakenly left the cash on the bed before taking a shower? Or did he really hire a prostitute last night and I was the only person who hadn't realized it?

I couldn't ask her and I didn't want to. She left me at the bar and went to bed with some stranger. She had taken something from me, from that day I was supposed to see Armin. She had done it on purpose. I imagined it all differently. I wanted sunshine, and breakfast, and Lejla without makeup. Naïve talk about *times past*. But the day was gloomy, like before rain, and those three hundred euros soiled its whole purpose.

'I had this totally crazy dream last night,' she said cheerfully, changing the topic as if she had just told me how to make cookies and not that she had beaten up Franz Josef for three hundred euros.

'I dreamed that I fell down the toilet and rolled all the way down to the sewers.'

'Aha . . .' I said. I kept looking at the money.

'There were some people there. In the sewers, I mean. A whole bunch of people. And they were all having a good time, like at a party . . . You know, well-dressed, suited up. And shit was floating all around us. And no one seemed bothered.'

'I'm gonna go take a shower. We've got half an hour left if we want to make it to breakfast,' I said and went to the bathroom. I locked myself in and sat on the cold tiles, staring at the scratched door. Did they go to another hotel or do it in this one? Did she like it? It was the first time we'd been apart since we met in Mostar. My ignorance bothered me more than jealousy, or some sense of morality. I didn't know what exactly happened. I didn't know who the woman in the bed was. Perhaps I had never known her. I wanted to go back to her seventh birthday and tell her that this freak, Lela Barun, would change her hair, and her eyes, and her whole being.

I wanted to go back to the river, where my best friend is screaming under some clumsy boy, and tell her – don't worry, one day they'll pay you to beat them up. I wanted to go back to the beginning, all the way to those paper dolls, and sit with someone else. Not because I hated her or judged her, but because I felt guilty. That little girl standing next to me, looking at the hole in the snow, at the crushed sparrow – she had turned into someone I didn't know. And I let it happen.

I tried to get up, but it felt as if I had forgotten how to use my whole body. I reminded myself where I was and why I was there. The bathroom is in the hotel, I thought. The hotel is in Vienna. He is here. The story will be over soon. I will forget all of her names. I will buy a charger somewhere and contact Michael. I will ask him whether he had found a pair of curtains. What our naked neighbor is up to. If he has finished that program. I will even ask about the avocado. That's important. I will tell him that Vienna was perfect, swollen like fresh bread. I will get on a plane and go back to his bed. It will smell of black tea in the morning, with some drops of rich milk. Nobody will mention Tito on my birthday. Michael will tell me, in Yoda's syntax, that *strong with this one the Force is.* We will order noodles, sit on the scratched parquet and watch TV shows. We will have sex on the dining-room table. A fight in the grocery store. His language. His guitar. His records. I will rest from myself and from her.

A long time went by. I couldn't move from the floor and turn the faucet on to at least pretend I was taking a shower. I didn't care what she would think. I could hear her in the room, rummaging through her things, spraying her hair. She didn't even bother to hide them, those three hundred euros. She left them there, on the table, as if she was proud of them, as if she had won them in a country fair shooting plush toys. Maybe it was just a misunderstanding, maybe I was overreacting. Franz Josef was an idiot; he paid for something that was free. He did strike me as someone who liked to pay for everything, even when it wasn't necessary, only to add market value to things and people around him. Lejla earned money from some dumb rich boy. *And* she got an orgasm into the bargain.

'Sara, you OK in there?'

'Yep. Yeah.'

'Did you fall down the toilet?'

'I'm fine, I was just feeling a little sick. No big deal!'

'Shit, we missed breakfast,' she said, 'but that's OK, we can eat something downtown. Now we can afford a fancy restaurant!'

I got up and unlocked the door. She was wearing jeans, with a big white bun on top of her head, standing in one sock. She smelled of apples. A little girl. Grownups pay her to punish them. She can punish me for free, for the *good old times.*

'I don't want to go to any restaurants,' I said.

'Ummm, OK. You wanna get a sandwich somewhere?'

'I don't wanna get any sandwiches. I want to . . . Finally . . .'

Words lay in my head like burning coals. I was afraid they would burn my throat if I let them out.

'OK,' she said.

'I mean we're here because . . .'

'I know.'

'I mean the whole point of the trip was . . .'

'I know, Sara. OK.'

'OK? OK what?' I asked. I was staring at the floor, at her sock, at the silver nail polish peeling off her toes.

'Put some clothes on,' she said. 'We're going out.'

I would be lying if I said I didn't enjoy the walk with her. We were surrounded by a foreign language, a foreign cathedral tolled its bells somewhere, and tourists crossed our path more than once. But at one point, when she ran in front of me to make it across the street in time, I remembered the black-haired Lejla running across the bridge on that perfect morning after prom. I remembered how we used to eat snow from the school fence and draw hopscotch in colored chalk on the sidewalk in front of her house. The biology teacher sprinkled rat poison in his garden and kept casting glances at us as we jumped on uneven squares and numbers. Lejla's foot would touch the line, which wasn't allowed, and she would keep jumping as if nothing had happened. But I kept quiet, proud in my moral victory. I remembered the choreography we came up with for a Janet Jackson song, once in her room. We would jump on *the stage* – the brightly colored carpet on the parquet floor – and count our steps dedicatedly eyeing each other, as if our entire future depended on that dance. Once we became teenagers, we pretended this had never happened.

This kind of small, stupid memory came to me and I realized that we would soon reach the last thread that connected us – her brother. I never once wondered what would come next; I was too busy imaging the scene, imagining adult Armin and me in his eyes. But now I realized this too would pass and once we established he was alive, something the two of us had known all along, there would no longer be any reasons left for us to call each other. We had ended on the island, I was well aware of that. The two tasks she entrusted me with after that – to bury Bunny and take her to Armin – were nothing but a sign of respect for our mutual history, not proof of friendship.

I was looking at that skinny woman with bleached hair and wondered whether that really was our last day, whether such things existed. We would run out of missing brothers afterwards, out of dead rabbits to give us some purpose. We would separate at last, like two heavy tectonic plates that have been moving towards different parts of the planet the whole time, though they were never aware of it. They thought of themselves as one continent for several millennia. *Lejla and I.*

I asked her if we should get a cab. She shook her head. 'It's close, we can walk. Half an hour tops.'

Then she stopped and approached me to get a leaf out of my hair. It was so badly entangled that she had to part my curls carefully to get it out of the vicious knot. She fixed my hair with her fingers.

'You're so pretty,' she said.

'Bullshit,' I said, which made her roll her eyes. She crushed the leaf and scattered its pieces on the sidewalk.

We kept walking slowly. St. Stephen's Cathedral stayed behind us. Lejla turned to small streets, her eyes down, looking at the cobbled paths.

I let her lead. If anyone could have taken me to Armin in that city, it was her. So I didn't complain when it occurred to me that all the little streets and alleys were just unnecessary detours from a simple line.

'Can I ask you something?' she said and stopped again.

'We shouldn't be late, I don't wanna keep him waiting.'

'We won't be late, we've got plenty of time left.'

'OK . . . What do you want to know?'

'Why did you steal Bunny that day?'

A group of Scandinavian tourists went by with long selfie sticks and enormous phones attached to them. For a second I had to bend my head in fear one of them would behead me. After they had photographed every single door and window and their reflection in them, they disappeared around the corner and we were alone at last.

'What do you mean *why?*' I asked. 'You told me to.'

'*I* told you to?'

'OK, you didn't *tell* me, but you gave me a sign.'

'A sign?' she asked in confusion.

'Come on, you remember . . . That guy, what was his name . . . Kraljević. He ran after the rabbits and we were left with the crate. You know . . . You looked at me like, I don't know . . . You gave me a signal.'

'Sara, I have no idea what you're talking about. You're crazy.'

She was doing it again. Mutilating my memories. We were so close to the end, a bit more and we were done. She could have left me one memory. Even Franz Bad Boy Josef was more generous. But I didn't want to fight. I kept walking down the cobbled alley.

'And that story you published in the *Literature . . . view . . .*'

'*Review,*' I said. 'I thought you didn't read my stories.'

'I read that one. About that man with black hair and a scar. The one that keeps walking in circles?'

'What about it?' I asked, pretending not to care. My temples pulsated as if ready to explode all over the pretty facades. Couldn't she just shut up and take us to the meeting point?

'That was Armin, right? That guy. The story is about him?'

'*That* was a literary character. You should know the difference, you studied literature,' I said more sharply than intended.

'So you can write a story about my brother, but not about me. God forbid such literary blasphemy.'

'As if you care whether I write about you or not.'

She just walked on quickly, her eyes glued to the street, and we made it to the main road. We passed an orange church and she spat her chewing gum at it. After walking in dead silence for a while, we came up to a huge building with a green statue of a horseman in front of it. The facade hesitated between light pink and beige. I squinted to read the name – *Albertina.*

'Here we are,' she said.

'Here? At the museum?'

'Are you coming or not?' she asked coldly and started walking up the steps. I followed her mutely. Besides, it wasn't that weird that Armin would be at a museum. He always loved art. He's sitting somewhere now, in some office perhaps, waiting for us to show up. He's wearing his favorite suit. He's holding his favorite ballpoint pen. He has a beard hiding his scar, but not entirely.

I followed her without question; she managed the complicated museum complex quite ably. At some point she told me to wait, climbed the red-carpeted stairway and approached a staff member to ask a question. When she came back, she told me we entered in the wrong part, we should have gone to the other one. I nodded, but said nothing. Anyone would have gotten lost in all those turns and passages.

Soon we were in front of a smaller gallery. She stopped before going in and gave me a worried look.

'I know,' I said, 'I'm nervous, too.' But she just touched my shoulder gently, as if to make sure she was accompanied by a real person, and went in.

It was dark inside. The wall was covered in dark-green wallpaper with the name of Albrecht Dürer printed in broad white type. There were only three paintings on show, but several people stopped there to study the works closely, while a stout guard was trying to get comfortable on a small corner chair. I saw in an instant that none of those people were him.

Lejla didn't say anything. She was waiting for a small group of visitors to move on to the next room, in order to get closer to the paintings. The last thing I felt like doing was staring at artwork I knew nothing about. Every now and then I checked the exits, starting each time a man walked into the room. At one point I thought I could see him, but that was impossible – I was looking at a frowning teenager in a black mackintosh. That's when I realized I would have to relax or at least try to look normal. If Armin walked in and saw us, I didn't want him to think I was stupid or bored.

I wanted him to think I understood art.

The paintings were small and, at first glance, simple. One showed a bird's wing in bluish-green plumage, the other was a sketch of adult hands joined in prayer. It was the third one that caught my attention. It showed a wild hare, with the artist's initials below it and the year 1502. The animal looked sad, its eyes seemed to have quit complaining and just given up. *All right, draw if you have to.* Dürer had drawn precise, yellowish-brown hairs in all directions. At one point the fur seemed to move, as if breathing. A tired, living hare in watercolors. My language has that mistake. We sometimes call rabbits hares, and hares rabbits, mixing it all up. But she never really had a hare. She had a white bunny, a fistful of life. We were wrong. A real hare stood before me, a true member of its kind. But something was wrong with that painting; something about it didn't make sense. I couldn't figure it out, no matter how much I stared at it.

I felt Lejla breathing next to me. Her eyes were lost in the hare's fur, as if she could see through watercolors and much further – through the wall behind the painting.

'You know,' she said, 'I shouldn't have slapped you. Then, on the island. I don't know why I did that. Really.'

'Lejla, what does it matter now?'

I looked around us again, but it was the same group of people from before. Were we early? Was he late? Was this the right room? But Lejla seemed assured, without hurry, calm in front of *Young Hare*.

'Have I ever told you he touched a Dürer?' she asked.

'You have. But I don't understand why he's not . . .'

'I was too little,' she continued, ignoring me, 'but my mom's told me the story a thousand times.'

My palms were going cold. The people around us turned into statues.

'Lejla.'

'Armin stood on tiptoe and touched the painting. But really – finger on the canvas. And then the whole circus kicked off . . .'

'Lejla,' I interrupted her. 'Where is he?'

Before I could realize what was going on, she lifted her index finger and touched the glass over Dürer's hare. No alarm went off, but one of the visitors shouted, 'Hey!' which made the guard jump off her chair, almost happy to have some purpose at last. Lejla seemed confused – she wasn't expecting glass. She wanted to touch the colors, hear the alarm. But then she saw the mad guard's purple face, some-one was telling the woman what had happened. 'Miss, I'm gonna have to ask you to step away from the painting,' she hissed in English and started coming towards us. Lejla looked at me just once. Her eyes looked tired, as if they were saying, 'Oh, it doesn't matter, I'll tell you some other time.' She ran out of the room and disappeared down the stairway, although nobody went after her. Even if they had, it wouldn't have mat-tered. Perhaps she was never very good at sport, but she could run wickedly fast. No one could run like Lejla Begić. I imagine she must have been outside the whole museum complex by then. She knew I wouldn't run after her. There was no point. The thread was finally broken.

I stood by the hare, I couldn't move. The man who had shouted 'hey' was now lecturing everyone on vandalism and the terror of our age and the new generations that have no respect for cultural heritage. The poor guard looked around her in confusion, not knowing what to do. 'She didn't really touch it,' I lied, 'I was here the whole time.' The woman just rolled her eyes, wiped her forehead, and went back to her chair shaking her head.

The room went quiet again and a new group of visitors entered. People were elbowing me gently in order to see the painting, muttering about how rude it was to block others. But I just kept standing there as if the hare and I were the only two beings in the whole museum, the whole city even. My body was very heavy all of a sudden. My joints hurt. I wasn't angry.

I wasn't anything. Had I been somewhere else, I probably would have started crying. It has always been the easiest thing to do to buy some time. But I couldn't do it this time; the hare wouldn't let me. I stared at the sixteenth-century watercolor feeling I would break and scatter across the floor in a million particles if I took my eyes off it. Everyone would see what I was made of.

A woman appeared in my peripheral vision and said, in English, 'Fascinating, isn't it?'

I nodded. I had no idea what she was talking about. My third-rate education never gave me the gentle sensitivity for fine visual art. I was looking at the painting because of a different hare. Who never really *was* a hare.

'They put it on show every ten years or so, I think,' she went on, 'it's so fragile and precious.' I couldn't locate her accent. At times it was pitch perfect, at times entirely off.

'Where do they keep it during that time?' I asked. My own voice surprised me. It came out old and hoarse.

'In complete darkness,' she answered, 'until it heals again.' Her *t* was hard, Slavic hard.

'*Heals?*'

'Yes. From light, humidity . . .' she explained.

I was looking at the picture wordlessly. Something still bothered me about it, something in it, *inside* of it, itched my brain, but I couldn't figure out what exactly. I felt extremely tired. And then the woman next to me said, 'And no one really knows how he did it. Whether he had a dead hare, or maybe sketched a live one in some forest, and then finished it in his workshop with a stuffed model.'

'It doesn't look dead.'

'Not at all,' she said, 'couldn't be more alive.'

'But a live hare wouldn't have sat still for the picture.'

'Definitely not.'

'And there's no forest,' I mumbled. 'No forest. Just empty space. No, actually. There's no space, either. He took it out of everything and just . . . painted it. He painted *a hare*.'

'Are you sure?' she asked. She was starting to annoy me.

'Don't you see there's nothing around it? Just empty canvas.'

The woman took a tiny piece of glass out of her bag and handed it to me. It was shaking in her wrinkled hand. That's when I looked at her. Her face surprised me. It was much older than the lilt in her voice, full of minute wrinkles around pale-blue eyes. Greasy gray hair fell in ugly strands over her big forehead. She reminded me of someone, but I couldn't tell whom.

'Look closer,' she said, 'into its eye.'

I took the small glass from her bony fingers and got closer to the painting. I looked through the magnifying glass. A little window was lit in the black, glassy eye. Dürer gave himself away on purpose. Did he really keep it in his workshop? Was it a reflection of a real window, or was that imagined too? Perhaps only the window had been real, and the hare around it was nothing but a skillfully reproduced memory. And maybe it was just a technique to make the eyes look real. But no, I thought. That's not the point. It didn't matter whether some hare from 1502 sat in one kind of space or another. Space was *within* it, within *the hare* in front of me, forever. Only painted hares have a *forever*. Living ones, flesh and blood, can't stand still.

The woman didn't rush me; she let me look at the artwork for a very long time. I had the feeling I was falling through the little hare eye. Nothing else existed anymore, just the darkness and in it – the reflection of a tiny window. After a while, I was certain I could see Lejla there. She was standing behind it, on the other side, trying to tell me something. No, not really. It wasn't *Lejla*. It wasn't *Lela*, either. Nor *Leja*. It was *you* that I saw in that window. You wanted to tell me something, surrounded by mute watercolors. Your lips were moving. I couldn't hear them, but I read them. They said: I only wanted